P9-EDX-840

DISCARDED

GABRIELLE

Mary Francis Shura

SCHOLASTIC INC.
New York Toronto London Auckland Sydney

No part of this publication may be reproduced in whole or in part, or stored in a retrieval system, or transmitted in any form or by any means, electronic, mechanical, photocopying, recording, or otherwise, without written permission of the publisher. For information regarding permission, write to Scholastic Inc., 730 Broadway, New York, N.Y. 10003.

ISBN 0-590-43133-1

Copyright © 1987 by MFC, Ltd. All rights reserved. Published by Scholastic Inc. SUNFIRE is a registered trademark of Scholastic Inc.

12 11 10 9 8 7 6 5 4 3 2 1   9/8 0 1 2 3 4/9

Printed in the U.S.A.   01

GABRIELLE

A *SUNFIRE* Book

SUNFIRE

Amanda by Candice F. Ransom
Susannah by Candice F. Ransom
Elizabeth by Willo Davis Roberts
Danielle by Vivian Schurfranz
Joanna by Jane Claypool Miner
Jessica by Mary Francis Shura
Caroline by Willo Davis Roberts
Kathleen by Candice F. Ransom
Marilee by Mary Francis Shura
Laura by Vivian Schurfranz
Emily by Candice F. Ransom
Jacquelyn by Jeffie Ross Gordon
Victoria by Willo Davis Roberts
Cassie by Vivian Schurfranz
Roxanne by Jane Claypool Miner
Megan by Vivian Schurfranz
Sabrina by Candice F. Ransom
Veronica by Jane Claypool Miner
Nicole by Candice F. Ransom
Julie by Vivian Schurfranz
Rachel by Vivian Schurfranz
Corey by Jane Claypool Miner
Heather by Vivian Schurfranz
Gabrielle by Mary Francis Shura

To the Showboats,
which have carried song and laughter
along America's Inland Rivers
since 1813

Chapter
One

GABRIELLE had been dreaming. The sharp rap of her father's knuckles on the door of her narrow cabin tumbled her back into reality with a painful start. With her eyes still tightly closed, she listened to the gentle slapping of the Mississippi River against the sides of the showboat and groaned. It couldn't be three in the morning yet; it absolutely couldn't. Yet above the rhythm of the current she heard morning sounds, muffled voices calling outside, and feet scraping along the decks of the *Levee Princess*. Within minutes she was supposed to be dressed and down in the galley to help Flossie McGregor fix coffee and breakfast for the other crew members before they untied the boat and started her on downstream.

Since her dream was fading too fast as it was, Gabrielle didn't even light the lamp.

Instead, she opened her window in the dark and let down her bucket on a rope. The bucket hit the river and filled swiftly, tightening the rope in her hands.

She pulled the bucket up and hesitated only a moment before pouring some of the water into her wash basin. If any silly little minnow had swum into her wash bucket, that was its hard luck, not hers. She washed her face and hands, and, after dumping the soapy water back into the river, she tugged on her pantaloons. Like all the cabins on her father's showboat, the room was narrow with only her bed, a shelf for her books, a washstand with pitcher and basin, and a row of shelves on the wall for her clothes. She had to twist carefully in the narrow space to reach the buttons down the back of her dress.

The memory of the dream was still more real than the darkness of her cabin. Her dress in the dream hadn't been ordinary blue gingham, but rose-colored taffeta, a deep, warm rose that flattered the vivid coloring she had inherited from her dead French mother: pale skin, hair as black as the wing of a crow, and brilliant blue eyes. The skirt of that dream dress had stood out like the flaring petals of a magnolia blossom as she bowed to a roar of applause filling the auditorium of her father's showboat.

And Stephen DuBois had been the first to rise to his feet, clapping. Stephen, who made a point of always having a job to do somewhere else on the boat when she came on stage to do her part in the show, would leap to his feet to start a standing ovation, a thundering ovation as she bent to the floor in one deep, graceful bow after another.

She stood motionless, thinking. If she could only talk her father into letting her try an act like that, her wonderful dream might really come true.

The rap came again at the door. "Coming, Father," she called. She lit the lamp a brief moment to brush her hair back and tie it with a ribbon. Then, before blowing the lamp out, she looked again at the poster someone had handed her at a landing near Pittsburgh, Pennsylvania. She had studied the poster so much that by now the paper was ragged around the edge. The rude handbill, just like the ones the *Levee Princess* distributed along the river, showed a girl walking a tightrope above the heads of the staring audience. COUNTESS ESMERELDA, it read, PERFORMING HER DEATH-DEFYING WALK BEFORE YOUR VERY EYES. She folded it into her pocket with an excited intake of breath. Her father *had* to at least let her try!

Out on deck, her breath formed a cloud of mist in the cold predawn air. There would be more warm days as they wended downriver between Illinois and Missouri, but this morning felt more like October than early September. Although birds were twittering in the willow trees along the bank where they were moored, it was as black as midnight out there. Aside from the glow of the lamp from the galley, the only lights anywhere were stars.

Gabrielle stamped a little on the stairway down to the galley. All right, she thought. So she was feeling sorry for herself, but she had a perfect right to. Nobody even knew what made that silly cook Jake Harwell mad enough to go packing off the boat at Hannibal, Missouri, without so much as a "fare thee well." One day he was whistling in the galley, and the next he was marching down the gangplank with his suitcase, leaving the galley full of dirty dishes for Flossie and her to clean up.

But showboat cooks were famous for being temperamental. Jake himself was the third cook her father had hired on since they started the trip in Cincinnati in April. If Jake had been there, she could have slept a few minutes more and brought the dream to its triumphant end.

But, then, that wasn't the only *if*. If she had been born to land people and lived in a regular house instead of on this boat, she could have slept for hours more. No other sixteen-year-old along the Mississippi River had to be up at three in the morning the way she did, especially after working a three-hour show that ended at ten o'clock. Even the round-eyed farm girls who came with their families and boyfriends to exclaim at the evening performances could lie in their beds until the sun was up!

Some day, she promised herself, some day

I am going to sleep in, too, and in a proper bed on land, not in a narrow cot fitted against the wall of a showboat cabin.

The galley air was fragrant with the rich scent of coffee boiling in the big blue-flecked enamel pot. "There you are," Flossie called over her shoulder. "The oven's heated up; you can get warm in here."

Gabrielle grabbed Flossie around the waist in a quick hug before getting down the coffee mugs. Flossie was not only wonderful, she was the closest thing Gabrielle could remember to a mother. She was also Gabrielle's only real friend.

Soon there would be biscuits to make, and bacon and eggs and potatoes to cook for the crew of nine who ate their regular breakfast later. Gabrielle couldn't wait that long. She split a leftover biscuit, buttered it, and stuck it into the oven to warm.

Flossie's husband Lance played leading man in all the showboat productions, and probably was handsome to people who could stand him. Gabrielle couldn't. She considered Lance a conceited dandy not worth the salt on his breakfast eggs. While Lance pranced around talking about acting and the theater as if he were Shakespeare himself, Flossie was the world's best sport. Even though she wasn't a day older than Lance, she was perfectly willing to play any role they needed, even if it meant powdering her beautiful red hair and making her voice creak like that of an old woman. Flossie had a

5

wonderful singing voice, but never complained at only getting to sing the old people's favorites, like "The Blue Alsatian Mountains" or Stephen Foster's "Old Folks at Home."

Gabrielle had been mad enough to spit when the cook had left. Flossie had only shrugged and said, "Gabrielle and I can manage until the captain can find us another." To see Flossie like this, with a gauze cap half covering her flaming red hair and her slim body hidden under a giant apron, no one would guess what a beautiful, talented woman she was. Now she hummed at her work, the snappiest sort of tune, as if to keep time with her hands.

Naturally Stephen DuBois had to come into the galley just as Flossie spoke. He poured himself a mug of coffee and blew away the steam, his dark, insolent eyes on Gabrielle. He turned to Flossie with a pained face. "I hope *she* isn't planning to make the breakfast biscuits. My stomach is still churning from the ones she made yesterday."

Gabrielle flushed and set two more mugs down hard on the table. You'd think an eighteen-year-old newcomer to the boat would have better sense than to pick on the captain's daughter. But Stephen seemed to know that Captain Prentice, appearing in the doorway, was too genial to take offense at anything that could be treated as a joke. He laughed at Stephen and patted his daughter on the shoulder in passing.

"Don't knock my girl's biscuits, DuBois," he warned. "I don't have my crew keeping guns handy by accident. More than one showboat has been attacked by ruffians along this river. Who knows? We could run out of ammunition and have to defend the *Levee Princess* by throwing Gabrielle's biscuits."

Gabrielle knew Stephen was watching her, gloating over her embarrassment. She didn't have to glance at him to know how smug and arrogant he looked, his smile strangely lopsided as if he was never more than half amused. How anybody that good-looking could be such a complete disaster totally astounded her.

A lot of her distaste for Stephen was just old-fashioned disappointment. She had been the only young person on board for a long time, which meant she didn't really have any friends near her age. It wasn't possible to get to know the young people along the river, even when the boat was tied up at the same place for a long time. The land people didn't see her as a real girl at all, but as an actress and singer. Then after the boat's dancer and acrobat left to take a job working on a Kentucky tobacco plantation, her father hired Stephen in Paducah. She had been really excited, thinking she would have somebody like herself on board the boat at last.

Had she ever been wrong!

Stephen was different, and better than most of the performers her father had hired on. He was not only a good gymnast and dancer, but could do an amazing number of other things. When the channel of the river was deep and straight, her father sometimes even let Stephen take the pilot's wheel.

And he was handsome, Gabrielle had to admit that. Most of the Frenchmen Gabrielle had seen in New Orleans and along the river were slender like Stephen, but not much taller than she was. Stephen was even taller than her father. His eyes, dark under black lashes, seemed to hide forbidden secrets. But she could certainly do without his smart mouth and his supercilious smiles!

When all nine of the coffee mugs had been handed out, Gabrielle took hers outside to join her father on the Texas deck. It was silly to call a deck after a state, but all showboats did it and the Texas deck was always the top deck with only the pilot house above it. Gabrielle settled herself at her father's feet as he and Pud Swallow watched the first glimmer of daylight come up above the Illinois shore and shudder across the face of the swift river moving toward them. Birds flew low over the face of the water, piping and crying. Now and then a bird went by standing on one leg to ride on the exposed surface of a racing log. From the darkness of the woods behind them, Gabrielle heard the barking of a coyote.

"They've had a real storm somewhere north of us," Pud said soberly. "Look at that current."

Although Pud was the funniest clown on the river and the best comedy dancer anywhere, he was a strangely solemn man. Gabrielle liked him as well as anyone she had ever known, except for her father and Flossie. He had prominent cheekbones, a large beak nose, and eyes set too close together. Without makeup he looked rather peculiar, but when he became a clown he was so perfectly right that she laughed before he even did anything. And like her father, Pud had worked on the river ever since the end of the War Between the States, and knew it as well as any man.

Her father nodded. "Maybe it's just as well it comes now. Those loose logs that struck us when we were tied up north of Hannibal left some weak places in our hull on the port side. The sooner we fix them, the easier the job will be. And you're right about the current, Pud. It looks downright hazardous. And it's not like we're rushed, either. We only need to make it downriver to St. Louis by the first of October."

As he spoke, a long row of barges pushed by the tug *Mandy Sue* passed them going south along the river. The quiet was broken by the greeting from the tug's engineer: one long whistle followed by a short one. The crew of the *Levee Princess* waved back from the deck.

"Griz is taking a chance even with that load he's pushing," Pud commented, lifting

9

his hand. Gabrielle waved, too. All the regulars along the river knew each other, as if the water itself were a moving town.

Gabrielle had recognized Stephen's distinctive light step coming up the stairs, but she ignored him. Of course, she thought, he didn't even have manners enough to stay out of a conversation between his older-and-betters.

"How long do you generally have to stay in at shore when the river runs high like this?" he asked. He had only worked on boats on the Ohio River before joining the *Levee Princess,* and the Ohio River was a bathtub compared to the turbulent Mississippi.

"It depends," her father said. "There's no sense in taking risks that will lose us more time in the long run. The flood stage could pass in a day or keep rampaging for a week. But as I was telling Pud, we won't waste the time we spend tied up here. We have maintenance on the boat to do, and maybe we could even work on some new acts for the show."

New acts. This would have been a perfect chance for Gabrielle to talk to her father about what she wanted to try, if only Stephen had taken his coffee into the dining room with the others instead of coming out on deck where he wasn't wanted.

"New acts?" Stephen asked. "That sounds interesting. Anything special in mind?"

I have something special in mind, she wanted to shout. Only Stephen, there in the darkness behind her father, kept her silent.

"I've been watching you, DuBois," Pud Swallow told him. "I like the way you handle yourself. I bet we could work up a comedy dance routine that would tip them into the aisles."

"Hey, Mr. Swallow," Stephen said, sounding very young suddenly, "I'd sure like that." Gabrielle stirred. He had better be impressed. Pud was the best comic on the river. Anyone who got a chance to work with Pud was privileged.

"Sounds good to me, too," her father said. "What about you, Gabrielle?" He touched her hair gently as he spoke. "Got any bright new ideas brewing? You added a lot to the band this year by learning to play that banjo."

"I *do* have an idea," she admitted, "but if you don't mind, I'll tell you later." As she spoke, she rose and took his coffee mug as well as her own. "I need to go help Flossie clean up."

"You and Flossie are a wonder," her father said gratefully. "Maybe we'll luck onto a new cook to hire at the next stop."

After taking Pud's mug, Gabrielle passed Stephen leaning in the doorway. She pretended not to see the empty mug he held out to her. Who did he think she was anyway, his personal maid? She might as well have taken it. He laughed in a low, teasing way that brought a furious flush to her cheeks.

Flossie was elbow-deep in hot dishwater when Gabrielle entered the galley. "Any sign of shoving off?" she asked, looking up.

Gabrielle shook her head as she slid the soiled mugs into the soapy water. "Father and Pud don't like the way the river is rising. They are talking about settling in for a while and fixing that place where the logs hit the hull up north."

"Do you know where we are?" Flossie asked.

Gabrielle shook her head. "Not exactly. I have a rough idea only because I looked at Father's river map yesterday. We're three days south of Hannibal on the Missouri side, but I don't know what town we're near."

"Probably not any," Flossie said. "There are more boat landings than towns along this stretch of the Mississippi. I was just wondering if there was a little town close or if we could find a farmhouse. We need to buy some salted side meat. I don't really have enough left to fix breakfast today."

"I'd be happy to go ashore and look for some as soon as it's light," Gabrielle told her.

Flossie grinned at her. "My goodness, child. I never knew a showboat person who liked going ashore as much as you do."

Flossie was right. Gabrielle did love going ashore. She especially loved going there in the early morning when the shrubbery along the bank gleamed with dew, and birds called from every bush. But this time it wasn't just being on land that made Gabrielle's heart leap. She would have to get money from her father. This would give her a perfect chance to talk to him about her planned act. She might even be able to start practicing on it this very day!

"I'll get some money from Father," she said, trying to hide her delight at the thought of an hour off the boat.

Gabrielle found her father alone in the pilot house, looking upstream through his binoculars. The map of the showboat's route lay open before him. As always, she leaned to stare at it. She loved looking at the rivers they had traveled, seeing the names printed in her father's clear hand. Wonderful names: the Ohio, the Kanawha, the Monongahela. When they reached Pittsburgh they came down the Ohio again, traveling a ways up the Kentucky, the Wabash, the Tennessee, and finally the Green River before reaching the Mississippi.

He lowered his glasses and smiled broadly at her before catching her shoulders in a hug. "You look at a map like a river pilot," he teased her. "Next thing I know you'll be wanting a showboat of your own." Then he remembered what she had said about the act. "You got me pretty curious down there on deck. What's hatching in that head of yours now?"

Gabrielle took a deep breath. "You have to promise me not to make up your mind too fast," she told him. "And remember when you look at this picture that I promise not to do anything dangerous. I just want to try something new in a way I have all figured out."

He was frowning before she even had the handbill out of her pocket. "You bet you aren't going to do anything dangerous," he said, his tone gentle. "You're all I've got, Princess. Out with it. What have you got there?"

His eyes widened as he studied the drawing of the young girl high above the crowd in a packed auditorium.

"Let me tell you how I figured it out," she said swiftly, knowing it was important to convince him before he said no and had to stick to it.

"Gabrielle Prentice," he broke in, "you could break every bone in your body."

"Listen, Father," she insisted. "It's nothing brand new. All my life I've heard about the Polish acrobat Madame Olinza. She did it on Spaulding and Rogers' *Floating Circus Palace* way back before the showboats all quit running because of the War. And I've figured out how to teach myself. I can start practicing on a broomstick stuck in the forks of a couple of trees. I'd begin just a few inches above soft ground and gradually work up. I wouldn't even try it above any hard surface like the wooden stage until I knew I was absolutely safe and you had seen me do it perfectly."

"Every bone," he repeated stubbornly.

"But I'm light," she reminded him. "I weigh hardly anything. And you know how good my balance is."

"But look at that woman," he said. "Up there in the air with those trousers on! It looks indecent, that's what. I don't know if you realize how hard it has been for me to build up the reputation I have. I give family shows where a man feels safe to bring his wife or sweetheart. And I never plan to do otherwise. Those pants of hers are downright vulgar. And don't start in on me about those bloomer girls. No daughter of mine — "

"Father," she wailed, "these are not the old days anymore. It's 1880. But, anyway, Flossie said you'd make a fuss about those pants, so we figured out how to make enough stiff skirts that nobody would even see my pantaloons from below. And you could bill me as Mademoiselle Gabrielle. It's not as fancy-sounding as a countess, but it looks good on paper."

"Tightrope walker." He frowned and fell silent for a long time. "Well, I will admit those circus-type shows bring in big crowds along the river. But Gabrielle, people work at learning that somewhere off in Europe. And just one fall on that wooden stage. . . ." His voice trailed off.

"I promise not to take any chances. Can't I just try? Not on the stage, but over soft ground. Maybe I won't even like it. But I just have to try!"

15

He studied her, his dark eyes thoughtful. Then he smiled and reached for her. "If you aren't the spit of your mother, Princess. She could never in her life settle for what she could already do. When we met she was a singer. Before I fairly looked around she was out-dancing everyone on the rivers. Then she took to writing those fine songs herself. No telling what she would be doing by now if the yellow fever hadn't taken her."

"Tightrope walking?" Gabrielle suggested swiftly.

He laughed softly, then shook his head. "I'd give a pretty penny if you were as easy to boss around as the rest of my cast. All right, give it a try. But remember, you're not doing it even one time on board this showboat until I know it's as safe for you as sitting in church."

She wanted to jump for joy, but held herself tightly. "Thank you so much, Father. I promise you won't be sorry." She paused and laughed. "Maybe I'd make a good gambler, too. I know enough to quit when I'm winning. While you're being agreeable, can I have a dollar?"

His face darkened at the word gambler, then he saw her grin and realized he was being teased. "Okay, Miss Mischief, what's this about?"

She laughed. "Flossie wants me to find a farmer who will sell us some breakfast meat while we're tied up here."

"Maybe you could wait a bit until the morning light is a little fuller."

"She doesn't really have enough to cook for breakfast," she told him.

He glanced at the Missouri woods behind the rude dock. They were still in deep shadow with the dawn barely breaking. "Maybe that young DuBois ought to go along with you."

"*No*," she said with more force than she intended.

His eyes were quick on her face. "Trouble between you young folks?"

She shook her head. "Not trouble. It's just that I don't need anybody."

He pulled a dollar out of his pocket and handed it to her. "Well, I need you, Princess, and don't ever forget it. And carry your knife with you. You never know what kind of crazy people you are going to run into on land."

Chapter Two

GABRIELLE went back for her woolen shawl against the cool morning air. The gangplank of the showboat was suspended a couple of feet above the sticky Missouri clay of the river bank. Once up north by Red Wing, Minnesota, the gangplank had been left down because some of the crew weren't back on board by bedtime. A young bear had wandered onto the boat in the middle of the night and scared everybody half to death banging around in the galley looking for food before they'd been able to run it off. Since then, Gabrielle's father ordered the gangplank hoisted off the ground a little at night, even if some of the crew had gone on land after the show was over.

She leaped down, landing with a soft thud. The yellowish mud of the bank bore the footprints of animals who had come for water.

She recognized the handprints of raccoons and sharp, triangular hoofprints of wild pigs. The woods *were* still awfully dark. The willow trees that blazed a clear gold in the spring light now had leaves as dark as the oaks and elms. The underbrush was thick and damp against her stockings. A deep-throated frog croaked before leaping into the edge of the river with a loud splash. When a bird she couldn't see screamed suddenly above her, she felt for the bowie knife at her waist, wishing her heart wouldn't thump like that at every noise.

Several rough paths led off from the dock area into the trees. She chose the one to the left because it looked more commonly traveled with fewer overhanging shrubs.

The woods were alive with the songs of birds. She always loved leaning on the deck rail and watching everything along the riverbank, but she loved the birds best. She only wished she could tell them apart, maybe even know one song from another. They hid so cleverly among the leafy greenery that she seldom saw more of them than a swift flash of color.

The woods gave way to an open pasture with mounds of drying hay here and there on the prickly golden stubble. Getting under the fence was easy, since it was only rude logs supported now and then by a brace. She located the closest farmhouse by a trailing wisp of blue smoke rising above another stand of trees. She had heard many stories, most of them supposed to be funny, about bulls. Since the stories had sounded more scary than funny to her, she looked carefully to see that the pasture was empty before she cut across it to reach the house.

A dog barked as she drew near, and a woman appeared at the door, shading her eyes against the sunrise behind the approaching figure. Gabrielle paused at the gate until the woman shouted the dog to her side, then she walked across the barren yard in swift graceful steps.

"Goodness," the woman said, smiling with delight. "You're the little actress from the *Levee Princess*. My, we did so enjoy that show last night." She paused. "Come on in, dearie." She led Gabrielle into the house without ever stopping to catch her breath. "That was an exciting play. For a minute there I thought my husband was going to take after that man with the mustache when he started mistreating you."

Gabrielle laughed. "It *was* only a play."

The woman paused and looked at Gabrielle, then reached out and lifted a strand of the waving black hair that had escaped Gabrielle's ribbon. "My! How pretty you are. They never seem like plays when they're going on. And the way he threatened you!"

Gabrielle smiled at her. "His name is Judd Harper and he's really a very nice man as well as being my friend."

"He didn't come off as very nice last night.

My heart was pumping until the hero came and got rid of him."

A dark-haired baby slept in a wooden cradle by the fire, and the warm kitchen smelled like cinnamon. So this is how it would be to live on land, Gabrielle thought wistfully.

The woman stood beside the cradle, too, staring at her child. "He's a boy," she told Gabrielle. "The fourth one in a row. I keep hoping I'll have myself a girl. Like you."

At the woman's insistence, Gabrielle sat on the kitchen bench and ate a cookie still warm from the oven. "I do my baking early, before it gets too hot," the woman explained. "I'm surprised the showboat isn't gone already. Usually they are off and downriver before we get up in the morning."

"The river is running high with lots of loose logs being carried along," Gabrielle explained. "It would be dangerous to leave while it's that way. Is there a town near here, in case we need more supplies?"

The woman nodded. "Only a few miles west. It's really a nice place, one of the nicer towns around, I guess." She smiled hopefully. "You might think of calling up another show if you stay over. I, for one, would pay to see it again. Sometimes it's a year or more between entertainments that my mister and I think are suitable for the boys. I like those songs singing in my head when I work."

* * *

With the side of bacon wrapped in a strip of muslin, Gabrielle started back toward the river. She stared into the woods as she passed. The trees were all shapes and sizes, some with heart-shaped leaves and others with murderous thorns and clusters of fruit that looked like tiny apples. When she saw two cottonwood trees standing a little apart in a clearing, she set the bacon in the fork of another tree and got out the poster she carried to look at again. In the picture the countess (wearing those pants her father had found so shocking, with a ruffled blouse and a top hat) was walking along a long, high rope carrying a parasol.

Gabrielle had to search a long time before she found a long, straight branch sturdy enough to support her weight. It was the matter of a few minutes to cut away the limbs with her bowie knife and make it into a fairly even pole. Since she didn't have a parasol, she chose a lighter, straight pole to use for balance.

The first time she couldn't even walk the pole lying on the ground. At the end of a half hour she had the knack of it. But the sky, which had brought early sun, was darkening. Let it rain, she thought. Rain would keep the river high! Let it really rain so she could come back and practice again and again. She couldn't wait to tell Flossie how well it was going. Maybe Flossie could even find her two broomsticks.

Flossie! She had forgotten all about the

time! They had breakfast to fix, and her father would be studying the river bank with a scowl. Worse than that, he might even send that Stephen DuBois after her.

She snatched the bacon from the tree and ran to the bank of the river to board the boat.

Flossie would find her broomsticks, she knew she would. Then all she needed would be two fairly matching forks in the trees and she could really start practicing.

Mademoiselle Gabrielle!

She could see the wonderful handbill Bony Rogers would print up as they started on downriver. Then let's see that arrogant Stephen DuBois walk out on her act with that sneering look on his face!

Flossie put the bacon on at once. It smelled wonderful, almost as good as the biscuits she had already rolled out before Gabrielle got back. She frowned as Gabrielle told her about the tree limb.

"You *will* be careful, won't you?"

"Oh, Flossie, don't you start that. You *do* have broomsticks, don't you?"

"No," Flossie said firmly. Her eyes twinkled. "How about mop sticks? Think they'll do?"

Gabrielle helped Flossie clean up the breakfast mess and got her to promise to tell only the captain where she had gone. With two mop sticks under her arms, Gabrielle started down the gangplank again. Stephen popped out of nowhere and stood staring at her.

23

"Lose something on shore?" he asked.

For once his tone was more curious than insolent. "As a matter of fact, yes!" she told him, starting off without looking back.

She *had* lost something ashore: her last doubt that she could learn to walk a tightrope if the river stayed high long enough for her to practice.

The rain came and kept coming. The supplies ran out and Flossie had to go clear into town to buy more. Although the river continued to rush by the *Levee Princess* in a murderous torrent, the sky cleared for a few hours every afternoon. Every day, as soon as that patch of blue appeared, Gabrielle leaped from the end of the gangplank and carried her mop sticks into the woods to practice.

She simply ignored the way Stephen Du-Bois stared after her, frowning sullenly. And her father kept his promise not to tell anyone what she was up to. But he couldn't hide his concern. "You aren't taking any chances?" he asked.

"With the ground this soft?" she countered. The ground indeed was soft, but she very quickly learned how to avoid falling. Every day she set the mop sticks higher, until, by the end of the second week, she had to climb the cottonwood tree to reach the forks where she set the mop stick she walked on. The stick in her hands worked every bit as well as a parasol would have. By carrying it with both hands, she could balance herself as she crossed the clearing on the strip of wood set higher than the top of her own head.

The river current began to slow on a Wednesday. That night the stars shone. "Another day like this and we can push off down-river," her father told Pud Swallow at break-fast.

Flushed with the excitement of her suc-cess, Gabrielle had already been tempted sev-eral times to ask her father to come to the woods with her. Since she could see how much she improved with every day's practice, she kept putting off asking him so she would be that much better. Now that she knew when he planned to push off, she could do her regular practice and then take him to the woods the next afternoon.

She had walked back and forth on the pole between the trees a half dozen times without wavering. Now that she had reached this point, she suddenly feared that what she was doing wasn't going to be exciting enough to be a real act. She practiced stopping halfway and then making a deep bow to the front with her right foot outstretched. When that worked, she tried it with her left foot. Her heart was pounding with excitement. She had it! She had a brand-new act to be writ-ten on the handbills and advertised ahead down the river.

She was rising from the deep bow with

her left foot in front of her when she saw him. He didn't seem to come. Rather it seemed that he had always been there. He stood beside an oak tree a few yards to her right, a tall, blond-haired boy with a deep, rich tan to his skin and eyes as blue as her own. He was staring up at her as if he could not believe his own eyes.

She stared back at him, startled, and felt her foot slip on the mop stick.

He moved quicker than a wild thing. He was instantly beneath her with his arms stretched up. One moment she was aloft with only the rustling of the leaves around her and the green scent of the woods filling her head. Then she was in his arms, being held very close with her heart beating fiercely against his and the scent of his face, like fresh air, against her own.

"Please, oh, please," she stammered, struggling to be let down.

Without releasing her, he studied her face for a long minute. Then gently, as if she were something breakable, he set her on her feet. His voice was surprising, very quiet but deep. "I didn't believe you were real," he said. "Now I don't know whether I want you to be real or not."

She felt the heat rising in her face and pressed down the skirt that his firm grasp had pulled all sideways. With a rush of horror, she realized he had to have seen half of her pantaloons, at least, and maybe more petticoat that he had seen in his entire life, except on a wash line.

"Thank you," she said breathlessly. "You scared me. That's why I fell."

"Have you any idea what I felt when I came through the woods and saw you there, up in the air as if you had flown?" He shook his head. "It's a wonder I didn't fall instead of you."

He was grasping her hands now, and Gabrielle knew she should pull them away, but couldn't bring herself to do it. She smiled back at him. "It must have been a shock. I'm really sorry."

He looked astonished. "Sorry? I didn't mean that at all. The minute I saw you I knew I had been waiting for just that moment my whole life."

What could she say to that? She dropped her eyes.

"Who are you?" he asked again. "Where did you come from?"

"My name is Gabrielle Prentice," she managed to say. "I came from the showboat *Levee Princess* down there at the dock."

"But where do you live?"

"On the river," she said. "On the boat with my father and the others." She tugged her hands away. "And I really *do* have to go now."

"You can't leave!" he protested. "Well," he said, replying to his own remark in that remarkable voice, "that's silly. Of course you have to leave." He caught her hands again and his words came all in a rush as if he had more to say than there could ever be time for. "But you can surely stay a little bit, just a little while. I couldn't stand it if I didn't see you again. I'm David Wesley. Tell me I'll see you again." He wasn't smiling anymore.

Why was she suddenly afraid? He had sounded as if he was under some kind of spell. Somehow she felt a little enchanted herself. She had this awful feeling that if she didn't pull away and run back to the boat that very minute, she would never be able to go.

She pulled free and, scooping up the two mop sticks, began to run awkwardly toward the river.

"Wait," he called after her. "Come back. You can't leave me now."

Her father was standing at the rail of the Texas deck beside the pilot house. The reflected sunlight flashed on the glass of his binoculars as he lowered them when she emerged from the edge of the woods. With his right arm, he motioned urgently for her to come. Steam was boiling out of the *Katie M*, the little tug that pushed the *Levee Princess*. That meant they were ready to shove off.

No, she wanted to tell him. No, not yet.

But he was calling to her, his voice strange across the stretch of wet riverbank. Stephen DuBois stood by the oak tree to which the boat had been fastened, ready to free the boat from the land by untying the rope.

"Hurry, Gabrielle, hurry!" her father called. "We're leaving right now in hopes we can make a few miles before dark."

When she glanced back at the woods, her father called again, his tone impatient.

"Hurry, Gabrielle, hurry."

Chapter Three

GABRIELLE'S father grinned as she ran up the gangplank. "There for a minute I thought I was going to have to send somebody to find you. I was even thinking of having Tom Luce signal you with a few bars on that calliope."

Gabrielle laughed, knowing he was kidding. No calliope player ever dared touch the keys of his steam piano unless the boat was going to put on a show. Calliope music carried for miles and the minute the farmers heard it, they began putting their tools down to come to the river.

Her father started for the pilot house, ducking his head to miss the line of wet clothing pinned on the lines strung across the deck. Gabrielle felt a rush of guilt. She should have been here to help Floss get the washing done. But it was too late to worry about that now. "Listen, Father," she said, skipping to catch up with him. "I thought you told Pud we were leaving tomorrow. I need to show you before we leave here. I'm ready, I really am."

For a horrified moment she feared he was going to ask her what she wanted to show him. He *couldn't* have forgotten. When he turned to her with a sober face, she knew he remembered about the tightrope walking. He was only putting it off because he was afraid for her. "We'll find a time for that, Gabrielle, but we've got to get into the current and try to work our way to the other side before another rain sets this river to boiling again."

She stared at him as he shouted the order for the tug to fire away. Why was she worrying? He never broke promises, at least he never had yet.

The throbbing of the engine in the *Katie M* grew stronger as she pressed her power against the *Levee Princess*. The larger boat lurched as it was nudged toward the center of the river. Wrinkles fanned out against the current. The trees on the Illinois side of the river seemed to rise and fall in a ragged line of green. The woods they had just left shimmered in the light, the call of song birds still audible above the pulse of the tug. Gabrielle stared back into that secret green. He was in there somewhere, that strangely attractive young man who called himself David Wesley. She could still hear his voice pleading, "Come back. Come back." She shivered from the memory of the mingled terror and excitement she felt as she had fallen into his arms.

Sighing, she turned to go down to the galley, where she would probably find Flossie singing cheerfully to herself while she went about her work.

The passageway was dark after the brilliance of the afternoon sun. Gabrielle blinked and almost ran into Stephen DuBois, who had posted himself right in the way and stood glaring down at her. Even when she paused and waited for him to stand aside, he didn't move.

"If you please," she said icily. "I would like to pass."

He stepped slowly aside. "What's your hurry? You sure haven't been moved to do anything but loll around on shore since we landed here."

She glared at him. He was impossible. Who did he think he was, criticizing what she did? It was none of his business. Somehow she was going to have to get through to her father how insolent and rude this man was. "Have you been appointed my guardian?" she asked.

"Nobody on this river would take on *that* job," he said. "Nobody but your father, that is. Any ordinary man would have yanked you back on this boat where you belong. Flossie is a fool to put up with doing your work as well as her own."

The mention of Flossie reminded her of the fresh washing hanging behind her. And already she could smell the rich aroma of food rising from the galley. Before she could think of a reply, he had turned and walked away, his footsteps crisp with disapproval.

Flossie was bent over the open oven door, her flaming hair drawn back with a sea-green cotton scarf. She smiled up at Gabrielle, her cheeks scarlet from the oven's heat. "How do you like the looks of those?" she asked proudly.

"Those" were three fat hens spilling brown masses of toasted cornbread dressing onto the long black roaster. The scent of sage and onion made Gabrielle suddenly ravenous. "Marvelous!" she said. "And they smell delicious."

"I hope I seasoned that dressing enough," Flossie frowned. "I bought the hens from a farmer lady for fifteen cents apiece. She had butter, too, and sold me a ham for only a dollar."

Another stab of guilt. Gabrielle always went shopping with Flossie and helped her carry the supplies home. "Flossie, I feel terrible about your doing all this work alone. How can I ever make it up to you?"

Flossie smiled, closed the oven, and sat down on the other end of the bench. "I've had fun thinking about you working on your act. How has it been going?"

"Wonderfully," Gabrielle breathed, almost

in a whisper. "I'm really ready. I was hoping to show Father today, but he got ready to leave too fast."

Flossie's eyes sparkled with excitement. "I want to see, too."

"Father has to approve it before I do it on the boat," Gabrielle told her. "And until then, it's still a secret."

"Do you suppose we could start on the costume?" Flossie asked.

Gabrielle hesitated. When would she ever get another chance to let her father see her act? "Maybe it's too soon. Father will never let me try my act over a wooden floor until he sees me try in a safe place."

Flossie put her arm across Gabrielle's shoulder. "Everything has its time. Your father didn't plan a show tonight because of the late start and the difficulty of getting over to the Illinois side in this current. It's like an extra vacation. But it's almost time to have supper. You might run down and see how you like the handbills for the next show."

Suddenly Gabrielle needed to tell someone about the boy in the woods. "Listen, Flossie," she began, her voice low. "I met somebody there on the land."

Flossie smiled warmly at her. "I know you did. That woman at the farmhouse where I bought the chickens and ham just raved on about what a pretty little thing you are and what a sweet way you have about you."

Someone was at the door. With her luck, Gabrielle thought, it would probably be

Stephen DuBois. She could only nod at Flossie before she escaped.

When Gabrielle was little, Bony Rogers had seemed like the oldest man in the world to her. Later, when she asked him his age, he gave her an answer she had to look up. "Halley's Comet came over the year I was born," he told her. "With Stonewall Jackson sitting in the White House as President." Since that had to be 1835, Bony was only forty-five now, even though he was as gray as summer dust and weighed little more than a boy.

Bony was working the old printing press in the corner of the dining room under the stage. Handbills were spread around him for the ink to dry while he pulled the bar forward over another sheet. "Hi, Purty," he said, grinning up at her. "You've been scarce as hens' teeth around here lately."

She sat down beside him and picked up a handbill. "I'm back now," she told him. "Let's see what you're cooking up for us."

Everybody on the boat did a number of different jobs and her father was no exception. Captain Prentice planned the programs for the shows as well as leading the band and performing as a magician and an actor.

The headline on the handbill was in giant letters: THRILLING EVENING OF ENTERTAINMENT! Gabrielle glanced over the program:

LEGERDEMAIN, SLEIGHT OF HAND

AND MAGIC! starring Captain Joshua Prentice assisted by Miss Gabrielle.

COMIC SONGS AND DANCES: Pud Swallow and Stephen DuBois.

"This act with Pud and DuBois is new," she told Bony.

He nodded. "Right good they are, too," he said. "I watched them practice during the rains."

The play was *The Lying Valet,* followed by Stephen's acrobatic display, then a love song by Miss Gabrielle, the "Sweetest Soubrette on the Stream."

"Bony!" she cried in protest. " 'Sweetest Soubrette on the Stream'?"

He flushed and ducked his head. "A man is entitled to his own opinion, even in print."

She rose and smiled down at him. "I suppose I will be carrying that awful armful of fake roses as usual."

He nodded. "Flossie tried to find you some fresh ones, but it's too late in the season. That's all right. They seem the same as fresh once you start singing."

Although the baked chicken and dressing were as good as they had smelled, Gabrielle couldn't get very many bites to go down. For the first time she could remember, she didn't feel a part of the laughing and jesting that went on around the table. She caught Flossie's eyes on her and began eating again so the meal would be over and she could get back up on deck.

Maybe everything seemed strange because it was so rare to have an evening moving down the river without a performance. Gabrielle went to the rail of the Texas deck to watch the Missouri landscape slip by. The green of the wooded shore deepened to a rich charcoal color after sunset. Against the ragged stripes of deep red and orange three hawks swayed in the air, their color lost in shadow. Once the boat was in the current, the motor of the tug shut off, letting the *Levee Princess* float without aid. In that silence, the sounds from the shore overwhelmed the lap of the water. Frogs and peepers battled in chorus against the endless sawing of the cicadas. Then fireflies began to wink in the darkness, high and then low, as if they were signaling.

Where did David Wesley live? Probably in a farmhouse, maybe like the one where she had bought the bacon — a farmhouse with a fragrant kitchen and a spotted cow in the barn lot behind. Were "lightning bugs," as her father called them, blooming in the pastures around David's house? Was his mind with her on the river as hers was with him?

Behind her the men's voices rumbled in talk. Politics, always politics, along with weather and the price of things. Everybody wondered how it would work when they moved the capital of Louisiana from New Orleans to Baton Rouge. Judd Harper's voice deepened with disapproval as he complained about the political conventions just past. "Too many political parties," he said. "Splitting the vote four ways makes it hard for a good man to get nominated."

"You might as well not count that Prohibition Party," Tom Luce, the calliope player, put in. "It'll come down to Republicans and Democrats again when the votes get counted."

"Like anybody knows who those candidates are," Flossie's husband scoffed. "James A. Garfield, indeed! Any man it takes thirty-seven votes to nominate has to be a nobody."

Captain Prentice stirred in his chair. "General Grant was a somebody," he pointed out. "He couldn't have done much worse as President if he had taken lessons."

Politics, always politics!

Gabrielle turned and went to her own cabin. She lay a long time in the darkness, thinking. She remembered David's words exactly: "The minute I saw you I knew I had been waiting for just that moment my whole life."

That was the most romantic thing she had ever heard in her entire life, even in a novel.

The following day was just like a hundred before it. After the three o'clock wakening, the *Levee Princess* started downstream at four, cutting carefully toward the Illinois side. Breakfast was served at ten to give everyone a chance to dress for the parade. About ten minutes before the *Levee Princess* reached the landing marked on the captain's map, Tom Luce went up to the calliope and began to play.

When the showboat edged into the stand about eleven o'clock, Gabrielle realized this was more than a simple boat dock. The buildings of the small Illinois town were visible down the path that led to the dock, and a small crowd had already formed on the beach as Captain Prentice ordered the gangplank let down and the boat tied up.

As director, Captain Prentice, in full costume, led the band down the gangplank and along the path that led to town. Only Pud Swallow and Stephen DuBois didn't play instruments. Both men, wearing striped clown regalia, did handstands and flips first in front of, and then following, the band. Dust rose from the unfinished street and dogs, frantic from the noise, lunged at the marchers' heels, barking wildly. A troop of barefooted boys in knee pants followed the dogs, shouting and mimicking the instruments in the band.

At the corner by the feed store, the band assembled for a free concert, during which Pud and Stephen cavorted through the crowd, handing out the printed programs. When a portly man with a handlebar mustache approached her father, Gabrielle guessed him to be the mayor. He would get free tickets for himself and his entire family.

The last selection of the free concert program was "Turkey in the Straw." As Bony

Rogers waggled his fiddle bow into the second chorus, a group of men pushed forward a young man of about twenty.

"You call that fiddling?" one of the men shouted. "Zach here could out-fiddle you with half the strings of his bow broke off."

"Fiddling contest!" someone shouted from the crowd.

Gabrielle ducked her head to hide a grin. Bony couldn't turn down the contest, but he would worry himself into a rag before fiddling the man down during the evening performance. He'd never been bested on the river yet. The closest he had come anywhere was once in Nashville, Tennessee, where the fiddlers had to draw straws to see who took him on.

"Yes or no," the man insisted. "Dare you face our Zach?"

Bony solemnly stuck his fiddle under his arm and reached out to shake the young man's hand.

"Show starts at seven," Captain Prentice called. "Don't be late. There's a fresh-minted gold piece for the winner of the fiddling contest."

As the cast walked back to the showboat with the army of boys still cavorting behind them, Gabrielle was thoughtful. Generally she didn't pay that much attention to land people. That day had been different. She had studied the faces of the young men in the crowd, wishing they were on David Wesley's side of the river. Not only was David not there, but not a single young man she had seen could hold a candle to his tall, fair good looks.

And it wasn't only David's looks. She loved the deep quietness of his voice and the intent way he had looked at her, as if afraid he would forget. She caught Stephen's dark eyes watching her as she mounted the gangplank and thought, with a stab of pain, of the almost reverent gentleness in David's face when it had been so close to her own.

Bony had stopped by the post office to pick up the mail, catching up with everyone as the gangplank was about to be lifted. As the members of the cast clustered about him to see if any of the letters were for them, Gabrielle slipped off to her own cabin.

Afternoons were free time. The men either amused themselves by fishing from the sunny side of the boat or going off to hunt ashore. Gabrielle and Flossie usually settled together on the cool side of the deck and read, sewed, or just talked quietly until time to get dinner ready to serve at four o'clock.

Gabrielle didn't even go out on deck. She lay in her pantaloons and camisole in the hot cabin, staring at the uneven boards of the ceiling. Was this how she was going to spend the rest of her life, searching the crowds that gathered in the towns along the rivers, looking for David Wesley's face?

She wanted to cry, but the tears wouldn't come.

* * *

Not until the dinner was cleared away and she was going off to dress for the evening show did Gabrielle even think to ask her father what song he wanted her to sing.

He laid his arm across her shoulder and smiled in a way that told her he was thinking of her mother. "I'm hungry to hear you sing 'Blue Sky, Still Water,'" he told her. That was his favorite of the songs her mother had written.

She leaned and dropped a kiss on his head. "Especially for you," she whispered.

As always, the evening became a noisy blur when the gangplank was raised at seven and crowds surged in. Whole families sat together, fussing over who sat by whom. Self-conscious young boys bought candy their girls didn't want from Bony, who passed up and down the aisle calling his wares at ten cents a bag. Young mothers rocked their restless babies in the flimsy straight chairs, trying to settle them down before the band struck up.

Gabrielle was there, but not there. She felt strangely withdrawn as if she was watching the performance from a great distance.

Her father got a rousing hand with his magic tricks, as usual. The fiddling contest threatened to go on forever before young Zach finally put his bow down with a rubbery arm, and his face streaming with sweat. The whole cast cheered him back to his seat.

The new act Pud and Stephen had prepared

stiffened her to attention in her seat. They were good, really good together. They started dancing seriously only to pick up speed until the dance turned into an acrobatic free-for-all that left both of them flat and seemingly dead on the floor. Their comic song, "The Ballad of the Lost Hawg," was almost as good. Pud sang his part straight with tears running down his face, while Stephen panto-mimed the fearful search and final sad ending. Gabrielle wiped tears of laughter from her eyes before they were through.

All right, Stephen was talented. She would concede that. He was rude and impossible and insolent, but talented.

For her solo, Gabrielle changed into a pale blue dress with a wide ruffled collar of lace framing her face. She walked slowly to center stage, carrying the awful artificial roses in her arms. She searched the audience a moment with her eyes and began. Something strange happened inside her as she sang the opening bars:

"I was a child and my heart was free,
Never a soul laid a claim on me.
Then in September my love walked by,
Blue was my heart as the evening sky."

The song she had sung since she was a child became more than words she had mem-orized to a plaintive tune. This was a cry from her mother's heart, a cry of love and longing, the same painful longing she had felt ever since she had run away from David Wesley.

She was unconscious of the sea of silent faces until the final bars. Then she bent in a deep bow, forcing herself to smile over the armful of garish roses.

For a moment it seemed as if all time stood still. Not a single pair of hands rose to clap. Many of the faces looking back at hers were shining with tears, and in the doorway, Stephen DuBois was staring at her as if she had grown a second head. She swallowed hard. What had she done? Had she ruined the show for everyone with her crazy mood? Then a storm of applause broke loose in the room. Several people rose to their feet. A lot of them blew their noses loudly while they stamped their approval. She bowed again and again as she fled to the side of the stage to escape.

The show was finally over at ten o'clock, with the grand finale bringing everybody to their feet.

From the rail of the Texas deck Gabrielle and her father waved at the crowd walking away to spread along the beach. The river nudged the ship's side and a half moon swung high above the darkened trees. Now and then a bird called or a horse whinnied a welcome to its owner.

Snatches of talk drifted back on the breeze. "That fellow sure can handle that fiddle," she heard. "And that little gal can tear a man's heart right out of his chest."

"That was quite some singing you did tonight," her father said quietly. His tone was strange and thoughtful.

She tightened her hand on his arm. "That was quite some song," she told him, knowing that wasn't what he meant.

She was glad to hear Flossie calling for her to help with the pickup snack for the crew. Gabrielle spread mustard and butter on bread for sandwiches with the leftover ham, feeling Flossie's eyes on her. When she glanced up, her friend's face was very sober. "That was what we call a dead giveaway, Gabrielle."

"I don't know what you're talking about," Gabrielle told her.

Flossie scoffed. "I've listened to you sing all your life. This was different. Something has happened to you, Gabrielle, something that has changed you."

"That's ridiculous," Gabrielle murmured, not knowing what else to say.

"Ridiculous love may be, my dear, but it's a fact of life. And it was there in your voice tonight. A man would have to be deafer than a stone in a raging current not to recognize the singing of a woman in love."

Chapter
Four

THAT next morning Gabrielle shivered awake in the dark cabin with a sense of unreality. Getting up, she lit the lamp and studied her face in the hand mirror that had been her mother's. The same old wide-set blue eyes stared back at her; the familiar nose that tilted up just a little at the end; the same cloud of dark, shining hair, spilling ringlets over her forehead.

"I haven't changed," she told herself. "I'm the very same person I always was. So why do I feel so strange, as if I were suspended, as if — as if time had slipped and wasn't working right?"

She seemed to hear David's voice, back in the woods, saying, "I have been waiting for just this moment my whole life."

That was it. She was waiting, but for what? To be startled again into that unaccountable mixture of joy and confusion that had now happened twice; once in her dreamlike experience with David Wesley, and then again with the stunned reaction of the audience to her mother's song?

Her fingers fumbled with the buttons down the back of her yellow-checked dress. She wanted to cry.

Twice that morning she went up into the pilot house, hoping to talk to her father about her new act. The first time he simply told her it wasn't a good time to discuss it. The second time that she whipped up her courage to go talk to him, Judd Harper was there talking about the way the river looked. She stopped at the door without even going in.

Strangely, Flossie gave her little or no sympathy. "Maybe you shouldn't be so secretive about it," Flossie suggested. "Perhaps if you just came out and talked about your plans in front of the other members of the cast, they could help you convince the captain."

"You don't understand," Gabrielle told her.

"Maybe I do and maybe I don't," Flossie said, turning away. Gabrielle studied her friend. It wasn't like Flossie to state things halfway like that. Had Flossie noticed how she was avoiding Stephen DuBois? Did she realize how humiliating it was to have those black eyes either laughing at her or staring coal-hard with anger?

Gabrielle didn't dare press Flossie to explain her words for fear she would have to come out and say how she felt about Stephen. Everyone else on board seemed to like him fine, and he had certainly proved his value to the cast all over again by his performance in the new act with Pud.

The day was hot. Black clouds of insects hovered above the shallows of the muddy stream and the bird songs from the passing shore sounded listless and uninspired. It was even hotter in the galley where Flossie sat sewing ruffles on a costume for her husband while keeping the stove going until it was time to start breakfast.

Gabrielle sat across the table from her, watching her needle flash in and out of the silken material. Flossie looked up at her in alarm as the boat suddenly lurched beneath them, rattling the pans hung along the wooden wall. "What's that?" Flossie asked, glancing at the clock. "It's only a little after nine, way too early to put into shore."

"Maybe we struck a sand reef," Gabrielle replied. "I heard Judd asking Father about a peculiar pattern the wind was making on the water."

"Oh, glory," Flossie said. "I hope nothing's gone wrong with this boat again!"

Gabrielle slid off the bench and ran up on deck. She saw the ruffles on the water that revealed a sand reef just beneath the surface. But they hadn't struck it. Instead, the

Katie M was nudging the *Levee Princess* toward the Missouri shore, where a rough wooden dock stood on piles between a couple of beached rafts. There were tying posts on the dock, which meant the boat could be fastened close to it. She wriggled her nose at the faint scent of skunk that hung in the moist, hot air, and went into the pilot house. Sometimes strange smells blew along the river, but none of them made her eyes water the way skunks and muskrats did. She waited behind her father until he had a free moment. "Why are we stopping?"

He looked over his shoulder at her and laughed. A band of sweat shone on his fine, high forehead and his shirt was open at the neck. "Because we're so popular. I should have reminded you this stop was only a few miles downstream. We won't have anything like last night's crowd — maybe twenty-five at most — but I promised them here that we wouldn't miss them on the way back downriver."

"Flossie and I haven't even started breakfast," she told him.

"No hurry," he said. "We'll have Tom fire up the calliope a little before eleven, then get off and play some music for the folks." That made sense. At such small landings along the river they didn't really put on parades, but just played some lively tunes on the beach, saving the real concerts for the towns that would produce larger crowds.

Gabrielle studied him a minute. "Father, since we have this extra time, maybe you can come ashore with me and see my act."

"Gabrielle," he said, a hint of irritation changing his tone, "it's not like you to nag. The right time will come for that, you'll see."

"But maybe I'll forget how to do it," she wailed.

He looked at her steadily. "If you don't have the act any better under control than that, we'd better forget the whole thing." Outside the men were shouting at each other as the rope was thrown, missed the post, pulled back, and thrown again. "Hey, cowboy, that's the ticket," somebody shouted as the loop of rope caught the post on the second try. The boat lurched as the rope tightened in place. Her father stood up. "Run on down and pour me a mug of coffee, please," he told Gabrielle. "I'll join you right away."

Gabrielle heard a thud as she passed into the galley, and wondered momentarily which of the crew had dropped something.

"Who's shouting out there now?" Flossie asked when Gabrielle had set her father's filled mug and her own on the long trestle table in the kitchen and slid onto the bench to wait for him.

"Some boy who was throwing rocks at the boat," Stephen DuBois replied, coming in as she spoke. "As soon as we got the boat tied he began yelling for the captain to put down the gangplank so he could come aboard."

"What's his business?" Flossie asked.

Stephen shrugged. "The captain went ashore to talk to him."

"He had to be watching for us to put to shore, because we sure haven't announced ourselves," Flossie pointed out.

Stephen nodded as he filled his own mug. "From what I heard, he was trying to talk the captain into giving him some work. I could have told him we were filled up."

"Except for a cook," Flossie corrected him.

"That guy is no cook," Stephen scoffed. "He's just a big, blond hayseed with a yen to get out of the cowshed."

Gabrielle picked up her father's coffee and started up on deck. Even if the coffee cooled before he came back to drink it, it gave her an excuse to get away from Stephen's scathing talk. Except for his obvious hero worship of her father and Pud Swallow, that fellow couldn't say a good word about *anybody*.

When she looked toward the beach from the Texas deck, she jumped, splashing hot coffee over the back of her hand. Her father was down on shore, standing near the end of the dock in conversation with a tall, blond young man.

David. David Wesley.

Without thinking, she pulled back into the shadow of the pilot house. Her heart pounded as if she had been running while she watched the two men. David was clearly talking a mile a minute, doing everything he could to convince her father. But her father shook his head firmly, and turned to come back on board.

As her father's feet sounded on the gangplank, Gabrielle stepped back into the pilot's cabin for fear David or her father would see her watching them.

For one breathless moment she got a full view of David's face looking up after her father. She caught at the edge of the door with her free hand. How tall and solid and fair he looked, standing there with his blue shirt open against tanned skin. The sun lit his fair hair like a candle. He was more than good-looking; he was handsome. But the disappointment in his expression made something hard and painful press against her throat.

"Your coffee's in here," she called when she heard her father's footsteps approaching. "What was all that about?"

"Good. Thank you," he said, taking the mug with a smile. "Just a nice country kid feeling the lure of the river. These kids don't understand there's more to working a showboat than being big and strong and willing."

"Everybody must have started somewhere," she told him.

He nodded. "But with an act. He's willing enough, offered to come along for nothing but bed and board. It wasn't easy to explain to him that a man has to pull his weight in the show as well as on board."

"Flossie hoped he would be a cook," Gabrielle suggested.

"I thought of that, but his answer wasn't satisfactory. I would guess he's got a mama out there who's never let him turn a hand in her kitchen."

He lifted his mug to his lips and smiled at her. "I will say he's willing. But I had to swallow a chuckle when he said cooking looked easy enough for a child to learn."

Gabrielle knew her smile was a little weak as she left. She paused by the pilot house, hoping to see David still on shore. But he was gone and Flossie was calling her to come help with breakfast.

In the next town, in order to use the handbills that had been left over, her father planned to give the same program they had presented on the Illinois side of the river the night before. The only change was Gabrielle's song. Without explanation, her father told her he was switching it to "Jeannie with the Light Brown Hair," which was the Stephen Foster song that Gabrielle liked the very least.

Gabrielle's coolest dress was made of pale yellow dimity. It was cut low at the throat and had a wonderfully full skirt. The waist nipped in with a flowered cummerbund, which Flossie tied into a butterfly bow in back so that the broad ends fell clear to the hem of the dress.

The heat that made Gabrielle listless also made her hair unmanageable. After three tries she gave up and let black ringlets escape onto her forehead from under the flowered ribbon that matched the sash of her dress.

Even if the auditorium had been full, she would have seen David at once. He was taller than most of the men, for one thing, and he was all alone, sitting halfway back so she could see his face clearly. Her heart dropped when his eyes met hers, and she fumbled with the tray of magic props she was holding for her father. How could she endure this? She stiffened her back purposefully and would not let her eyes stray to that part of the audience again.

Gabrielle had never lived through a longer evening. The simplest things were suddenly difficult. She fought to remember the lines of the play she had rehearsed and performed a hundred times. The sense of waiting had changed to something more terrifying, something like dread. She felt as she did on those spring days when the skies darkened suddenly and the air grew heavy in warning of a coming storm.

If her father had thought changing the song would change the audience's reaction to Gabrielle's singing, he was wrong. Although she didn't even *like* that song, she heard her voice turn wistful and haunting as the audience stilled to a breathless listening.

Only when she bowed to the floor in response to the roar of applause did she meet David's eyes again. She gripped her flowers hard, suddenly dizzy for no reason.

But the three-hour performance was finally over, with the grand finale ending with a roar of applause. It was common enough for members of the audience to come forward to congratulate the players, but David was there too quickly, seizing her hand.

"We have to talk," he said quietly, that deep voice as gentle as she remembered. "I tried to get on board earlier."

"I know," she whispered. "I know."

"I can't leave you," he said. "You know that, don't you?"

She knew without looking that the other members of the cast were watching this little scene from the corner of their eyes as they nodded and spoke to people in the crowd.

"We can't talk here," she whispered.

"I'm not letting you go again," he replied.

Fighting a sense of panic, she smiled past him and began to walk from the auditorium, with him following just behind her. Here and there she stopped to accept praise from people rising to leave.

When they finally reached the deck, David pulled her toward the shadow of the pilot house.

"Listen, Gabrielle," he whispered, seizing her by both shoulders, "I haven't thought of another thing since that day. I fought with my mother and came down here to see you. I love you, that's what. I love you and I mean to have you."

"But, David," she stammered, "you don't know me and I don't know you."

His voice turned almost rough. "What's the matter with you, Gabrielle? Haven't you ever heard of love at first sight? Tell me you haven't been thinking about me."

His grip was so tight on her arms that she didn't dare try to move away. "David," she implored softly. "Make sense, please try to make sense. . . ."

"To make sense you have to have some," a voice broke in. Stephen DuBois, still wearing the scarlet tights and jerkin of his acrobatic act, was suddenly there, shoving himself in between her and David. He grabbed David roughly by the shoulder and spun him around. "Now look here, guy. There's no fooling around with *this* girl. Get off this boat before I throw you off."

"Stephen," she cried, grabbing at his arm and throwing him off balance.

Pressing his advantage, David squared off and struck Stephen a hard sudden blow to the shoulder that sent him reeling backward against the door of the pilot house.

Stephen's eyes blazed as he came back, his lean body in a half crouch. "You hayseed!" he cried, leaping at David.

"Hold up!" Gabrielle's father shouted as Stephen lunged for David. "Back off, Du-Bois. You there, get off this boat. Start moving."

David, still in fighting stance, shook his head, his eyes watchful of Stephen.

"Move," Captain Prentice repeated. As he spoke, the other members of the cast lined up behind him — Judd Harper, Pud Swallow, and even Tom Luce the calliope player, who only joined the other men when it pleased him. Gabrielle had seen this happen before, seen a troublesome land customer have to be thrown off by the cast working almost as a team. This was different. David wasn't drunk and he wasn't carrying a gun or knife as most of the troublemakers did. The men moved steadily toward David as Stephen stood back, watching in silent fury.

"Move," the captain ordered again.

"Listen, Father," Gabrielle cried. "This is a man I met on shore. He's not here to cause trouble."

He looked at her, plainly astonished, then snorted. "Well, he *has* caused trouble and I want him off this boat." He turned to David. "You have a sporting choice. You leave or we throw you off."

David looked along the line of men, straightened his shoulders, and turned toward the gangplank.

"One other thing," the captain said quietly as David walked away. "You're not to bother my daughter anymore, understand?"

Gabrielle wanted to call to David as he walked down the plank toward the beach, where the remnants of the crowd had stopped to watch the fight. They watched him silently until he had passed through their midst and disappeared. Captain Prentice signaled for the gangplank to be lifted.

"Father," Gabrielle cried.

"Another time," he told her, turning away. "We'll discuss this another time."

The rest of the men left the deck one by one, without comment. In the silence that followed, the music of the shore swelled in volume: the cry of the peeper frogs, the calling of night birds, wisps of talk and laughter from the scattering crowd now hidden by the darkness of the trees.

Only the memory of David was left, disappearing alone into the edge of the woods. Gabrielle folded her arms around herself, holding the places on her upper arms that still tingled from his grip. This was what she had been dreading, the end of that dream that had begun when she had glanced down from her heights in the trees and saw him looking up at her.

Behind her came the slap of a hand on a mosquito. She jumped and turned to see Stephen leaning against the outer wall of the pilot house, watching her. His face was hidden in the shadows as his voice came low and furious.

"So the mystery is solved," he said acidly. "That's what you were doing during those days ashore — adding one more man to your string of lovesick admirers. Don't you know that there's an ugly word for women who lead on every man they meet? Do you think your father deserves *that* for a daughter?"

She gasped, unable to believe his words.

"Oh," she said furiously. "Oh!" She gathered her skirt and tried to dart past him into her cabin. He was too quick for her, catching her by the shoulders and holding her fast.

"You can't stand the truth, can you? The sweetest soubrette on the stream, are you?"

"You're hurting me," she said in a furious whisper. "Let me go or I'll scream."

He was very close, as close as David had been that day in the woods. She felt his hands loosen on her arms but stood staring at him, unable to believe the anger in his eyes. When he dropped his hands, that mocking half smile came to his lips.

"That's funny," he said. "It didn't seem to hurt when that farmer had hold of you."

She stumbled running down the passage, blinded by tears and rage.

Chapter Five

WHEN Gabrielle went down the next morning to give Flossie a hand with early coffee, her friend looked at her curiously. "I thought your father was making excuses for you, but I guess he could be right."

"Right about what?" Gabrielle asked.

"You *do* look mighty peaked. When you didn't come join us all for the late snack after the show last night, he said you might be coming down with the shakes."

Gabrielle reached for the mugs and set them on the table. "That's ridiculous. I've never gotten that river fever in my life and you both know it."

When Flossie only shrugged, Gabrielle went on. "Quit acting so innocent. You know I didn't come down because of that silly scene Stephen DuBois started after the show."

Flossie's pale, delicate eyebrows rose. "Stephen started?"

Gabrielle flushed. "He *could* have minded his own business."

"One thing about a showboat crew," Flossie said genially. "If they think one of their number is in trouble, they take it as their own business. I have been personally glad of that a few times."

"Oh, Flossie, stop it!" Gabrielle said crossly. "You know this wasn't like that at all. David is a boy I met on shore. I liked him and he must have liked me because he followed the boat down here to see me again. We were talking privately when Stephen broke in and started that fight. Father wouldn't even have noticed David except for Stephen. And now Father has told David to stay away from me forever." For a dreadful moment she was afraid she was going to cry. She pressed her palms against her face to hold back the tears. Flossie's arms were tight about her at once.

"Then you really like this boy?"

Gabrielle nodded, clinging to Flossie tightly.

"That's a different kettle of fish altogether," she said briskly. "Splash a little cold water on that face and we'll put our heads together on it."

Gabrielle stared at her in disbelief. "Flossie! You mean it?"

Flossie grinned at her, the mischievous

grin that was all it took to remind Gabrielle of how much she had always loved Flossie McGregor.

"Hey!" Flossie said. "I was a girl once myself, a little schoolteacher in a one-room schoolhouse just out of Nashville in Tennessee. I met Lance when the showboat stopped on the river. It was like a bolt of lightning for both of us. You know Lance. I knew what my brothers were going to think of him, but I *would* have him in spite of all."

"So what did you do?"

Flossie tightened her shoulders and giggled. "I borrowed my brother Smoky's fastest horse and followed the boat downriver to the next stop. I had my head wound with flowers and the captain was performing the wedding ceremony when Smoky and my little brother Lem came storming onto the boat with loaded guns. That stopped the wedding, you better believe. They took me back home and watched me like a burning fuse on a dynamite cap. You see, with my mother and father both gone, Smoky thought it was his duty to raise me up right."

"But you *did* marry Lance, finally!"

"It didn't take all that long," Flossie said airily. "After they brought me back I wouldn't do anything. I wouldn't teach school or even get dressed to go try. I just sat in a chair in my room and wouldn't eat or sleep or talk to either of them. Neither did I cook for them, I might add. They threatened and shouted and called Lance a dandy and a fop and puppet and every other ugly thing they could think of."

Gabrielle swallowed a smile. In truth she had thought the same words about Lance McGregor herself.

"Men are short on patience," Flossie went on. "My brothers soon got fed up, hitched a buggy, and tracked the boat to a landing. Smoky gave me away and swore he had never made a better bargain in his life." Flossie stopped and covered her mouth with her hand. "Glory!" she breathed in a stunned tone.

"What's the matter?" Gabrielle asked.

"What am I doing, telling you all this? You mustn't try any such tricks. Your father would kill me."

"*My* father?" Gabrielle challenged her.

"Well, he'd make me wish I was dead, anyway. But just hold tight. We'll work this out, you'll see!"

The clouds shut out the blaze of sunlight a little after eight that morning. By breakfast they hung so low and heavy Gabrielle felt as if she could reach up and touch them. "We'll be lucky the rain doesn't drown out our parade," Captain Prentice said at breakfast.

"Most of us are neither sugar nor salt," Stephen DuBois said quietly.

Gabrielle took a deep breath and almost choked on her bite of egg. Smart Alec, that's all he was. Maybe she wasn't the *sweetest* singer on that river, but *he* was sure the one with the most obnoxious mouth.

Although the little town had only dirt streets, it was a sprightly looking place with several stores along the main street and an ice-cream shop that advertised sandwiches in the window.

The rain began to patter softly just as the concert wound down. Flossie opened the big purple parasol from the boat to hold over Gabrielle and herself.

"I have a mind to shop awhile before coming back on board," Flossie told the captain. "Do you mind if Gabrielle comes along to keep me company?"

Gabrielle fumed at his quick, suspicious glance. Did he think David Wesley had nothing to do but lie in wait for a girl he had been forbidden to see? Or did he, like Stephen, think she had become a vain girl who collected lovers along the river like beads on a string? "That's fine with me," her father said grudgingly. "But watch you stay dry. There's always summer pneumonia."

"My father is getting to be an old hen," Gabrielle grumbled as they watched him start back to the boat with the rest of the cast.

"Your father loves you with all his life," Flossie replied.

Flossie bought a piece of cotton yard goods with lilacs splattered all over it, and enough matching purple linen for a big wide sash. "I can see you in this," she told Gabrielle.

"Especially in spring when we can get lilacs for you to carry on stage." Gabrielle found a tiny, heart-shaped box just the right size for the ruby ring her mother had left her. They had shopped for about an hour when the heavy clouds let loose a downpour that drove them into the ice-cream parlor.

A small bell chimed over the door when they entered. The place was cheery with candy-striped wallpaper and matching chairs at tables for two or four people. The steamy air smelled of cream and chocolate.

Gabrielle was halfway through her hot fudge sundae and Flossie was describing the lilac dress she was going to make, when David's shadow fell across their table. Without asking, he pulled a chair from another table and sat down between them. When Flossie stared at him, Gabrielle felt a rush of scarlet come into her face. "Mrs. Lance McGregor," she said hastily. "I'd like you to meet David Wesley."

Flossie nodded but had no time to reply before David seized Gabrielle's hand and leaned close. "He's not going to get away with that, you know," he said earnestly. "We are going to be together no matter what your father says."

"Mr. Wesley," Flossie put in.

He didn't seem to hear her, but went right on speaking directly to Gabrielle, his eyes intent and pleading on her face. "You see, I love you. No force in the world can stand in the way of true love. We were *meant* to be together, Gabrielle, and that's how it's going to be."

"Mr. Wesley," Flossie said, a little more loudly this time.

"If we have to run away together, that's what we'll do," he told Gabrielle firmly.

Flossie, her bright eyes snapping, took her spoon from the table and cracked David's hand with the back of it. He stared at her in astonishment. "Mr. Wesley," she said quietly, "I am the closest thing Miss Prentice has to a mother. I feel it my right to ask you to contain yourself and be a little clearer about your motives."

"Motives?" David asked. "Why, I want to marry her, of course."

"Glory," Flossie said with a groan. "Have you asked her if this is what she wants?"

Strangely, his lips tightened and his cheeks flushed a little. "I haven't had a chance to until today. You see," he said, now leaning toward Flossie, trying to explain, "the minute I laid my eyes on Miss Prentice, I knew I had made a big mistake in having an arrangement with Mollie Thompson."

Flossie let out a long breath. "Then you are already engaged?"

"Oh, no ma'am," he said quickly. "I used to be, but I'm not now. You see, after I met Gab — Miss Prentice, I knew I'd made a mistake, and told Mollie so."

Flossie could have had a mop stick for a spine, as straight as she sat up. "And your Mollie took this in good spirit?" she asked.

"Oh, yes," he nodded. "Mollie's an easy-going, very nice girl. We've known each other all our lives. She understands me."

"And you two live around here?"

He shook his head. "No, it's more like ten or fifteen miles upstream, where you were docked when I first met Gabrielle."

"Then how does it happen that you're here?"

"I borrowed a horse from home and have been following the *Levee Princess* downstream. I camped and waited on shore while you did that show over in Illinois. I don't intend to go home at all until I can take Gabrielle with me."

"And what do your parents say to this?"

His face darkened again. "There's only my mother. She *is* excitable and got pretty upset, but she'll settle down. It's a matter of giving her time."

"Glory," Flossie said weakly, leaning back in the chair.

When David looked across at Gabrielle, she felt that awful melting feeling again. He was crazy, but crazy in the way lovers were in novels. "Will you marry me, Gabrielle?" he asked gently. "I can't offer you much else right now. I do have an acreage Grandpa Harper left me that we can build a house on. Any kind of house you want. All I want is to be with you always."

When she stared at him, still stunned beyond words, he put the question again. "Don't you want to marry me, Gabrielle?"

She shook her head helplessly. "David, I don't know. You don't know me and I don't know you. How do we know that we will love each other enough?"

"I love you enough for the both of us," he said quietly.

The rain had let up and then begun again, sweeping against the glass windows of the shop. The bell tinkled as the door opened, letting in a sweep of water and cool air.

Flossie's voice was suddenly strange. Her question was not so much whispered as breathed aloud. "What does Mollie look like, David?"

He turned to her, startled, then glanced toward the door, following her gaze. Two women, their bonnets darkened with rain, stood just inside the door. They were a study in contrasts. The younger one had a round, doll face framed by golden, sausage-shaped curls springing out from under a pink bonnet. The older one wore her hair in a dark knot caught at the base of her neck. She was glaring through round horn-rimmed glasses at the table where they sat, her brows knit with anger.

"Mother! Mollie!" David cried, springing to his feet.

In deference to David's mother's age, Flossie and Gabrielle both rose also. Mrs. Wesley crossed the room like a stern-wheeler, with Mollie tugging along behind her. When David hastily pulled up two chairs, his mother sat stiffly with Mollie at her side.

"Never mind standing," she said to Flossie and Gabrielle. "Acting the part of a lady makes no difference in what you really are."

Gabrielle gasped, feeling as if she had been slapped.

"Mother," David said reproachfully.

"You stay out of this," she told him without even glancing his way. "You have established, by your actions these past days, that you are temporarily out of your mind. Or bewitched," she said, pausing. "I cannot believe that less than dark arts could have led an honest, loyal, loving boy from his hearth and home."

Gabrielle had watched the slow rising of Flossie's fury. She was at her most dangerous point, past careful choice of words and not yet to shouting. "How old is this boy of yours, madame?" Flossie asked sweetly.

Mrs. Wesley had the grace to look mollified. "That is of no concern," she replied. "The history of man is replete with examples of honorable young men having their heads turned by sirens and temptresses."

"Madame," Flossie warned.

"Mother, please!" David tried again.

Gabrielle leaned toward the older woman, her voice as low and calm as she could keep it. "Mrs. Wesley, I am neither siren nor temptress. I am a singer and actress on my father's showboat. I have used no dark arts on your son. We met and he has followed our boat downriver — "

"Stealing a horse," his mother broke in.

"He gave me to understand the horse was from your stable. I couldn't steal from my father," Gabrielle told her quietly. "If I had need of something, he would give it to me freely."

"Need," the woman repeated. "What he needs is an old-fashioned horsewhipping to put some sense back in his head."

Flossie flew to her feet. "I have heard enough. Come, Gabrielle, we have no call to sit here being insulted by a woman who has no more respect for her own dignity than she does for that of her son. My sympathy to you, David."

She had Gabrielle by the hand, practically pulling her along. When the proprietor started from behind the counter to follow them, openmouthed, Flossie tugged a coin from her purse and tossed it to him. It struck the wooden floor and rolled a few feet before clattering to a stop.

"Flossie," Gabrielle gasped as Flossie struggled to open the parasol against the rain. "That was a five-dollar gold piece."

"A person doesn't quibble on price in the company of villains," she said tartly. "Come along, love, I want to see you safely back on the river."

Flossie said nothing during the preparation of the evening meal. She turned the breaded catfish carefully in the hot fat and laid them in a golden row on the platter.

Gabrielle shivered now and then, and felt the strangest sense of loss, almost like pain. She shoved a giant cut cabbage down the sides of the grater to make coleslaw. Only when the platter of fish was in the oven staying warm and the rest of the meal ready to serve, did Flossie sink to the bench with a sigh.

"Glory!" she said. "There's nothing like getting up a good mad to give me energy. Tell me, Gabrielle, do you love this young man?"

Gabrielle shook her head helplessly, fighting to hold back the tears that hadn't come when she needed them. Flossie's voice rose as she took Gabrielle's hand. "Why am I badgering you? I heard what you told him. How can you know if you love him when you don't even know him? No more than he knows you, like you said. So that's the first problem right there — getting you two together."

"But you heard his mother!" Gabrielle wailed.

"So she's excitable," Flossie said. "She was talking when she should have kept shut. She could learn a thing or two from that Mollie-bump-on-a-log. She just sat there smiling like a jack-o-lantern the whole time. Whew!"

"And I told you what Father said," Gabrielle reminded her. "He said — "

"I know, I know." Flossie lifted her hand tiredly. "Just let me deal with it. I used to think I was being put upon to be raised only by my brothers. I'm beginning to think there's no easy way to grow up, no matter who's there to help you."

The show was sold-out in spite of the rain. The audience reminded Gabrielle of the groups who came down in the bayous of Louisiana. Since so many Cajun people understood only French, a steady whispering went on all through the show as friends and relatives translated the words to each other.

But these people weren't having any language problem. They were just all busy gossiping. The whispering was always followed by people staring at Gabrielle. Her neck and shoulders ached from the tension of holding her head high. That silly little town! The story must have been carried from one end of it to another by the time she and Flossie got back to the boat. Never mind them, she told herself proudly, they were land people and couldn't help being the way they were.

They finally all left with their staring and their eager whispers. The cast had cold sandwiches in the galley and went off to bed. The boat had been quiet a long time when Gabrielle, lying awake in her cabin, heard a soft rap on her door.

Flossie, her red hair loose almost to her waist, tucked her white wrapper around her legs and sat on the edge of Gabrielle's bed.

"The captain agreed to let you and David get to know each other," she said in a careful whisper.

Gabrielle sat straight up and stared at her. "My father? He agreed to that?"

Flossie nodded soberly. "He said he'd write a letter to Mrs. Wesley the minute I left. He's inviting David to travel on board with us, maybe as far as St. Louis if he wants to."

"Flossie!" Gabrielle threw her arms around her friend and leaned a long moment against her breast, listening to the calm, even rhythm of her heartbeat. "But how?" she asked, looking back into Flossie's face. "How did you ever talk him into it?"

Flossie shrugged as mischief played across her face. "Promise you'll never tell Lance!"

As if Gabrielle ever told Flossie's pompous husband any more than the time of day!

"I threatened to leave the boat."

Gabrielle stared at her. "You didn't!"

"I certainly did, and he didn't like it much. He pointed out that I might not get another job so easy along the river without Lance. I told him if Lance wanted to stay with him, that was all right, that I could probably do as well getting another job as he could do getting along without a cook."

"Flossie!" Gabrielle giggled behind her hand.

"You've heard that old saying that there are more ways to tame a cat than by choking it with butter?" She rose, smiling. "The same can be said of men."

Chapter Six

IN payment for his trip to the local post office, Bony collected a dime from every cast member who received mail. Gabrielle usually paid no attention to what he picked up from general delivery addressed to the *Levee Princess* because no one ever wrote her a letter, anyway. That changed when she learned about her father's letter to Mrs. Wesley, inviting David to travel with him. In fact, she had difficulty concealing her eagerness until he could reasonably expect an answer.

"But how will she know where to write to Father?" Gabrielle asked Flossie.

"He probably gave her a list of the places on the Missouri side that he means to stop at," Flossie told her.

After the next performance on the Illinois side, they wakened to a deep river fog. No matter how hard she strained, Gabrielle couldn't even see the silhouettes of the trees along the shore. Her father called such a fog "a peasouper." An eerie silence fell. With the boat traffic stopped by the fog, the familiar melodic whistles stopped, too. The boat seemed to rock in its private cloud, the silence broken only by the occasional splash of a leaping fish or a chorus of grumbling bullfrogs along the shore.

There was nothing to do but wait. It was silly to wash clothes because they wouldn't dry in the wet air. Flossie, unable to get fresh supplies, prepared strange meals of whatever she found in the pantry. Up on deck the men whiled away the time playing cards and talking about what they'd seen and done. Pud Swallow had actually seen Jesse James at a landing in Missouri, and Tom Luce had a friend in Northfield, Minnesota, who had gone to see the Younger brothers when they were jailed after a murderous bank robbery there. Gabrielle fled back to her cabin, knowing that such stories would give her nightmares.

Not until the third morning did the fog lift enough to permit the boat to start on downriver. After a brief concert on the beach, Bony went into town for the mail. Gabrielle could hardly bear the suspense when she saw him hand her father a slender envelope. He stared at it, slit it with his pocketknife, and pulled out a single handwritten sheet of paper. The moment he looked up at her, she knew David was not going to get to travel with them.

"I tried, Gabrielle," he said quietly. She felt her heart tumble. Her father could at least have told her he was sorry, even if it wasn't the honest truth. "I really did try," he said again.

"That's all right, Father," she said, keeping her voice as calm as she could. "I guess I really didn't expect her to let him come."

"She gave a good enough reason," her father said. "They're going into harvest on the farm and he's needed to help." As he spoke, he folded the sheet of paper again and slid it back into the envelope before putting it into his pocket.

"The captain did his best," Flossie reminded her when Gabrielle told her about the letter. "That's more than I hoped for when we started this."

Gabrielle nodded and went back to her cabin.

She lay a long time on her stomach across her bed, even though she knew her gingham dress was soft from the hot humid air and would wrinkle like anything. In all honesty, she wasn't surprised. What she had told her father was true. She *hadn't* really expected that woman to let David come. But just knowing it was all over, with no hope left, made her feel tired and very heavy, as if every part of her body had suddenly turned to lead. Maybe she did have the river fever

— "the shakes," as her father called it. She was even tempted to pretend to be sick for a week or two. She wouldn't have to dress up and smile and speak lines and sing when she had nothing in the whole wide world to sing about.

From the deck above she heard the friendly rumble of the men talking together. Flossie was probably sitting with Lance, finishing the fancy shirt she was making for him while he spouted off one of his pompous lectures about the theater. As soon as Flossie finished that shirt, she planned to start sewing Gabrielle's lilac dress.

Gabrielle wished Flossie would forget she even had that material. She could do without anything that would remind her of that dreadful day and that awful woman. Well, almost anything. Gabrielle smiled ruefully to herself. Hot fudge sauce poured over vanilla ice cream still sounded good.

She flopped over, smoothed her dress with her hands and stared at the ceiling, feeling the comforting rhythm of the boat rocking from the waves of a passing steamer. How could something — no, someone — come in from the outside world like David had and take all the pleasure out of her life? She was surprised that she didn't even feel like crying. Instead she felt limp, wondering how she was going to stand the days ahead, even the years with nothing to look forward to and no energy at all.

"All right, Gabrielle," she told herself

sternly. "You've always claimed to be an actress. Let's see how good you really are. You have to act as if nothing has changed, as if you were not walking around with your heart absolutely smashed flat."

The show played to a full house that night and the next. The weather stayed hot even for a Missouri September. Things that Gabrielle never paid much attention to before drove her wild: the clouds of mosquitoes that circled the boat at sundown, waiting to pounce on any square of exposed skin; the smell of fried meat hanging in the stale air of the galley; the way people told her the same stories over and over as if she was deaf or had no memory.

The third day after the letter came, Stephen DuBois caught her alone in the galley. His dark eyes were angry as he blocked her way. "How long is this going to go on?" he asked.

"I don't know what you're talking about," she told him. "Get out of my way."

"She doesn't know what I'm talking about!" he said in an exaggerated manner. "Don't you realize we are all sick and tired of watching you mope around like the dying princess in a bad play? Those manners of yours — so polite, so careful to smile even if you don't mean it."

"Get out of my way. What I do is none of your business."

"At least that was honest," he said. "Now

why don't you try being honest with yourself about that hayseed of yours? You're just lucky to be rid of him. He's nothing but a mama's boy. He wouldn't last ten minutes in a real man's world."

She wanted to hit him, to shout at him, to knock him out of her way. But then, what did his hatefulness matter now?

"Thank you, Monsieur DuBois," she said acidly. "Now that you've given me my lesson for the day, *GET OUT OF MY WAY!*"

He flushed at her tone. "That's only lesson number one, and there's lots more where that came from. Try thinking about somebody besides yourself for ten minutes — like your father, for instance. You've even managed to get him down-in-the-mouth, although why he cares is beyond me."

Then, with a sarcastically courtly bow, he stepped back and let her pass.

She walked on quickly without looking back. He was hateful, but his words had hit a sore nerve. She had tried not to see how soberly her father watched her when he thought she wouldn't notice.

She was doing her best, trying her hardest. What more could she do?

When everyone was turning in after the next night's show, her father called as she started toward her cabin. "Come sit with me on deck awhile."

She groaned inwardly. Was *he* going to give her a lecture, too, the way Stephen had?

She couldn't bear it if he did. But neither would it help to hurt his feelings by not going out to sit with him. "Let me get a shawl against the mosquitoes," she told him. "I'll be right up."

Once on deck, Gabrielle sat on the floor and leaned against her father's knees as she had since she was a child. He was obviously having trouble thinking of things to talk about. He talked about the moon and the show just past. Then a voice spoke behind them. "Mind if I join you?" Stephen DuBois again! At least, she thought resignedly, she wouldn't get a lecture with him around.

Her father sounded relieved as he gestured to Stephen to join them, explaining that they were just enjoying the cool night air. Then he stirred in his seat and his voice trailed off. A stern-wheeler was moving downriver, carefully holding to the deep channel of the water. Her high decks gleamed in the full moonlight as a dense flurry of spray from the wheel behind her rose in a cloudlike wind-driven snow. The *Levee Princess* began to bob gently on the waves of the steamer as the steamer's whistle signaled her passing. Captain Prentice shook his head.

"Sitting here in comfort like this, it's hard to remember how dangerous these boats are. They are really nothing more than fancy barges tricked up with trimmings and smoke-stacks."

"But dangerous, Captain?" Stephen asked.

Gabrielle's father laughed. "Let's put it this way, son. I've had one blow up under me, two set on fire and burned, and three of them snagged and taken down. You can't say that for many front porches."

"It's a wonder you stay with it," Stephen said.

Gabrielle's father grunted. "No man chooses where he's born or where he dies. It's only fair that he gets to choose where he lives in between." As he spoke, her father laid his hand on Gabrielle's shoulder. She held very still, but words simmered in her mind.

A man might get to choose, but what about a woman? Somewhere back up the river David could be looking at that same glowing moon. Would he be thinking of her and seeing her as clearly in his mind as she saw him?

Finally Steven rose and bid them goodnight.

Her father didn't move. "Sleep well. We'll be going along in a bit."

As soon as Stephen was gone, her father's hand tightened on her shoulder. "I better talk fast before we get interrupted again. I've been thinking about that act of yours. I plan to pull into a little country landing early tomorrow. How about we take that time for you to show me this tightrope business?"

Gabrielle gasped in disbelief. "You mean it, Father? Oh, how wonderful!"

"Keep your voice down, child," he cautioned. "This is still a secret between the two of us. You are sure you'll be ready?"

"I'm ready," she assured him. "I'm *really* ready."

Gabrielle felt Stephen watching them the next morning as she and her father walked down the gangplank to the beach, her father carrying the mop sticks in one hand. There her father stopped. "Didn't you tell me we needed a patch of woods with some good-sized trees?"

When she nodded, he motioned her to a path that led to the left. Her father saw the perfect trees first. He frowned and fitted the mop sticks into the forks of the trees for her. "Now how do you figure to get up there?" he asked.

"I climbed the tree before," she told him.

His frown deepened. "That would be a problem on the boat. Do you think you can do it on a slant?"

"I don't see why not."

He took down one of the sticks, set it in a low fork, and left the other high. "See? This way you could step on low; do the act to the top; and then come back down and jump off in a good, deep bow."

She grinned at him. "My father, the showman!"

"Don't sell the old man short. Were you thinking of doing this to music?"

She nodded. "I just couldn't decide what song would be best."

"Give it a try and I'll watch your rhythm."

Her heart thundered. This was her chance, she thought, maybe her only chance! Oh let it work — let it work like magic!

The first few steps were uncertain, but she quickly picked up confidence. When she reached the top and turned, she came down a step, did the two deep bows she had practiced, and ran swiftly down to where her father stood.

"Bravo!" he cried, his voice hoarse with emotion. "Bravo, my child." He caught her and held her close for a long minute. Something in the way he clutched her was frightening. She pulled back and looked up into his face.

"You're not kidding me. Are you sure?"

He grinned. "I couldn't be more sure. I'm just having an inside tug-of-war. The father in me is panicked for your safety, but the showman in me tells me you have created an act that will make the *Levee Princess* the most welcome entertainment on the river. A real winner." He paused. "When do you think you could have a costume ready?"

"I'll have to ask Floss."

He unhooked the mop stick from the tree and caught her arm. "All right, Mademoiselle Gabrielle. How do they say it? A star is born?"

"Could we still keep it a secret as long as possible?" she asked.

He nodded. "I'll have to tell Pud so he can help figure out how to string the ropes up good and tight. And Bony will have to know so he can put the act on the handbills. But they'll keep mum."

Wonderful, marvelous Flossie. Gabrielle watched her empty the costume trunk on the bed and start stacking petticoats together. "I know they need a press," Flossie said, "but start pulling them on, anyway."

With the sixth ruffled petticoat in under her full skirted dress, Flossie cried out. "Look at that! Not a sign of those pantaloons above the knee!"

Gabrielle's father strung a short length of the rope across his larger captain's cabin so she could practice with the different feel of the flexible rope. To her delight, it was actually easier and more fun than the solid wooden stick had been.

The secret excitement of the coming act infected all who knew of it. The show was in better shape than it had been for several nights — more lively, with more bounce to the music. She gave the poster to Bony to look at, and he walked away thoughtfully. When he came back, he showed her the picture he had made. The girl looked as if she were dancing high on a long line with a parasol in her hand. In his picture, she had top billing with the tightrope walker poised above the rest of the program.

As usual, a crowd gathered early on the beach, drawn by the strains of the calliope. The band was assembling on deck to go down the gangplank when Bony came up from the press with an armful of the new handbills.

Stephen DuBois glanced at the top bill, muttered something gruffly, and seized the piece of paper. "You can't be serious!" he cried, turning to Gabrielle. "This is the craziest thing I ever saw in my life. Who do you think you are?"

"Now wait a minute," Captain Prentice said, turning to face him. "What's your problem, Stephen?"

"This!" Stephen shouted, pointing to the picture of the girl on the tightrope. "She could cripple herself for life — kill herself, even."

"Hold it right there," Gabrielle's father told him. "You know I wouldn't take any chances with any actor on this boat, my own daughter least of all."

"But, Captain — " Stephen replied, his eyes blazing.

"*Captain*," Gabrielle's father repeated firmly. "That's the key word, DuBois. I am captain of this showboat. If I approve an act, no one second-guesses me. If you don't like the act, leave the show."

For a stunned moment, Stephen stared back at Captain Prentice. He turned very pale. Then, without another word, he nodded and took his place in the band formation for the parade.

Dinner was over. Gabrielle, dressed for the performance in her stiffly starched and ironed petticoats, went to the auditorium to try the ropes for the last time before actually doing it during a show.

Stephen entered the room so quietly that Gabrielle didn't know he was there until she turned at the top of the rope and made her first deep bow. She caught her breath, remembering that day in the woods when she had been startled by David. But David's face had been filled with wonder. Stephen stared up at her with anger and fear. She looked away, and finished her descent with a deep bow on the floor.

To her surprise, he was there at once. He reached down, took her hand, and drew her to her feet. "That was excellent," he said quietly. "It's amazing that you could learn that without an instructor, but you must not do it."

"Not do it?" There was no end to his cockiness.

"Not do it," he repeated. "You could do it five times or twenty, and then something would happen. The rope could give, you could have a moment of dizziness. I beg you, Gabrielle, change your mind."

"But the handbills are already printed," she reminded him, unable to believe this conversation.

"Then burn the handbills and tell the people there was a mistake."

In the grip of his intense feelings, he had seized her hand and was pressing it hard.

She studied him thoughtfully for a moment before speaking. Why was he so bothered? He had heard her father's opinion. "Tell me, Stephen," she said quietly, "why does it make so much difference to you?"

To her astonishment, he flushed a deep, angry red and dropped her hand. "Your father," he said after a minute. "I don't think the captain realizes what a blow it would be to him if anything were to happen to you."

He turned and walked rapidly out of the room, leaving her staring after him.

Chapter Seven

BY six o'clock, a full hour before the show would begin, the beach was already crowded with people waiting to get onto the boat.

"It's that tightrope-walking business of yours," Flossie told Gabrielle crossly. "I wish I had never encouraged you to do it."

Gabrielle stared at her in amazement. "I would have done it, anyway."

Flossie caught her lip in her teeth and shook her head. "Glory! You're right. You probably *would* have done it, anyway, but I didn't have to make it easier for you to kill yourself. I keep forgetting how much you are like your mother!"

"How can you say that? You didn't know my mother," Gabrielle reminded her.

"I've heard enough stories to feel that I did," Flossie replied. "Bony says when she got some idea in her head, you might as well just stand back. She would go straight through a brick wall, if that was what it took."

"That's not a very nice thing to say about anybody," Gabrielle told her.

"It depends on whether the thing really needed doing or not," Flossie replied. She rose and went to look at the gathering on the beach again. "There's no way your father can fit all those people in this boat."

"Oh, but he has to."

Flossie shook her head. "Sooner or later, but he doesn't have to do it tonight. He can always promise to stay over another night to accommodate them. He'll probably pass out marked handbills to be sure the people who waited out there tonight are the first ones to be let in tomorrow."

Gabrielle looked thoughtfully at the crowd waiting on shore. "You know, Flossie, it always amazes me that people will stop their work, hitch a buggy, and drive all this way to pay good money for only three hours of entertainment."

"That's just because you've never lived like they do. Some night you should go on the beach where they are and look out at a showboat from the land. The darkness out there stretches as far as they can see in every direction. Even the face of the river flows dark except when the moon is full. Then a showboat comes in and lights up the world like Christmas, and spangles the water with light. The music of that calliope sets their hearts to thumping a new beat. There's color and excitement as long as the show lasts, and the twang of banjos and jokes and songs to remember when they go back to cows that need milking, plows that have to be pushed, and long dark evenings when they can't even read because they need to save the kerosene."

"Is that how you grew up, Flossie?"

She nodded. "I remember living for special things — a wedding, even a funeral. Oh, sometimes we had a barn dance or some of us young people got together to make taffy or play games. But deep inside I was always waiting, restless and hungering, for something glittering that I knew was out there somewhere. I didn't even know where it was until I walked up the gangplank and saw my first show on the river."

"And that's when you fell in love with Lance?"

"I think I fell in love with the magic of the showboat first. Lance was the part of it that loved me back and offered me a way into his world. We were married better than a year before I could even think of him as an ordinary man, like my brothers or the boys I grew up with."

Gabrielle fell silent. She wanted to ask Flossie if David could possibly see her like that — not as a real girl, but as a glittering part of a world more exciting than his own. Oh, but he couldn't. Not the way they had met. There had only been the two of them.

He hadn't even known at first that she was a part of the showboat.

Her father called from the door of the auditorium. "Cast in place for opening act."

"If you are the least bit scared, you don't have to do this," Flossie said swiftly.

"Quit putting fears in my head," Gabrielle told her.

Usually by the time the band started, the beach was dark and empty, with the people already settled in their seats in the auditorium, waiting in silence for the opening strains of music. That night was different. Voices filtered into the auditorium from outside. Some of the sounds were angry. Gabrielle glanced around the stage. What in the world was going on? Two of the men were missing from the band: Pud Swallow and Stephen DuBois. Her father lifted the baton and the music began, drowning out the angry fighting sounds with the lively strains of "Turkey in the Straw." By the time the band filed off to leave the stage free for her father's magic act, Stephen and Pud were back in their places, in costume for their act, which was to follow.

Her father had scheduled Gabrielle's new act as the last event before the grand finale. When the time for her act came, she was shivering inside. Too many people had told her to be careful. She had had too much time to look along that thick rope stretched above the benches and rows of seats filled with staring strangers. At the highest point of the rope she would be so far above the heads of the people that if she fell. . . .

"Stop that," she told herself fiercely. All her life she had heard show people talk about having "butterflies in their stomachs" on opening night. Whatever flopped under her tightly cinched belt felt more like turkey buzzards. She was hot and cold by turns, and had trouble making her breath come regularly.

But it was time.

Her father had chosen an old Robert Burns ballad as the music for her act. Flossie had first said she would play the accompaniment on the dulcimer, but later decided she was nervous enough for Gabrielle's safety without having to think about the notes, too. Judd Harper executed a brisk roll on the drums. Bony, his fiddle under his chin, nodded to Gabrielle and pulled the bow across the strings.

The tempo of the music was perfect. As the first strains filled the room, Gabrielle stepped onto the taut rope, whirled the small scarlet parasol, and began her slow ascent.

She deliberately shut the audience from her mind. She concentrated on the song, its tender melody, and touching words:

"Flow gently, Sweet Afton, among thy green braes. Flow gently, I'll sing thee a song in thy praise."

Bony had never played so beautifully. And never had he played to a room so silent. When

Gabrielle reached the high point of the rope, pivoted, and slowly turned, low gasps came from the openmouthed faces below.

She was doing it. It was working!

A swift curl of exhilaration ran up her spine and she smiled with delight. First a bow to the left foot, and then a bow to the right. As the final notes of the song ended, she ran swiftly down the rope into her father's waiting arms.

The tumult of the shouting, stamping, cheering crowd made her ears vibrate. People were out of their seats, pressing toward her. Her father clasped both hands about her waist and lifted her onto his shoulders. "Smile," he whispered up to her. "Smile at them and wave!"

Before she met David she had dreamed of a triumph on stage, a triumph that would even bring applause from Stephen DuBois. From her father's shoulders, as she threw kisses to the crowd and smiled until her face hurt, she looked for Stephen. She finally saw him at the back of the room, leaning against the wall, not even clapping. He seemed sad — sad and different. As she looked at him he turned, his hand over his right eye, and slipped out the door.

The audience finally settled down enough for the cast to come out for the grand finale. When Gabrielle came forward to bow, the wild cheers and stamping began all over again.

"What did I tell you, child?" Her father

whispered with delight. "You are a star!"

The people filed out noisily, their voices lively with praise and excitement. Flossie's stage makeup was streaked with tears, and even Lance, who passed out compliments as rarely as if they were hundred-dollar gold pieces, bowed over Gabrielle's hand and said, "A vision of loveliness. My tribute!"

Then she heard the sounds of angry voices again and realized the audience was still milling on the deck instead of filing off down the gangplank. Gabrielle's father strode swiftly from the room with Judd Harper right at his heels.

"You again." She heard her father's voice raised in fury. "We had more of you than we mean to take. Lend a hand there, men."

"What's going on?" Gabrielle asked.

Lance shrugged. "Some farm kid tried to fight his way onto the boat before the show. They threw him off but he can't seem to understand the word *no*."

Farm kid. Gabrielle stared at him and rushed to the stairs to fight her way through the crowd to the upper deck. When the customers saw who she was, they stepped back to let her through. She reached the top of the gangplank just as Judd Harper, along with Stephen and Pud, dragged a shouting figure down the gangplank and onto the beach.

"David!" she screamed.

He turned at the sound of her voice and would have tried to fight his way back to her if the men had not held him by both arms.

"David," Gabrielle moaned to Flossie, who had followed right behind her. "Why are they treating him like that?"

Flossie caught her arm. "I didn't want to bother you before the show, but he raised an awful ruckus trying to get in after the seats were sold out. The minute they put down the gangplank again, he was trying to bully his way up here."

Gabrielle stared at her. They were all against her, every one of them. Her father, even Flossie, who knew how much she cared. Gabrielle pulled free of Flossie's grasp and ran into her cabin, slamming the door behind her. As hot as her mass of clothing was, she threw herself across the bed, not even caring if she cried her eyes red and her face all puffy. To her astonishment, no tears came. Her eyes felt hot and dry, and the trembling came back.

Maybe she was too angry and hurt to cry. Maybe crying was something you could only do about unimportant things. This was important. She had been betrayed by the very people she loved and trusted the most.

She lay in the darkness, numbly listening to the sounds of the boat being shut down for the night. When it was time for the late supper, she heard her father call her name softly outside the door. When she didn't reply, he opened it just a little. She kept her face turned away as a slender shaft of light fell across her bed. She hoped he would think she was asleep. He stood there a long moment, then closed the door and went away.

Flossie came and sat on the bed, her hand warm through the back of Gabrielle's blouse. "Your father did what he thought was best," she whispered. "Try to realize that the captain only did what he thought was best."

Gabrielle struggled to keep her breathing even. She didn't open her eyes until Flossie sighed, rose, and went away.

Gabrielle couldn't remember ever lying and listening so long after everyone was asleep. Some of the sounds were the same as during the day: the soft slap of water against the ship's side, the creak of the tying rope as the boat fretted against its mooring. Other boats signaled in passing, one with a low, sorrowful whistle that hung and wavered in the air. From the land came the living night sounds: the plop of a diving animal, the hum and screech and racket of a night insect chorus.

But sleep didn't come. She undressed in the dark, stacking the petticoats on her single chair. Wearing only a light wrapper over her gown, she walked up to the Texas deck, setting her bare feet down carefully to keep the old boards from creaking under her weight.

At the rail, she leaned to stare at the shore where David had waited, then tried to come to her only to be fought back — not once but twice. How could the people who said they loved her be so cruel to someone they knew was important to her? She hugged her arms tight and, for the second time in a single evening, actually wished she could cry.

The sound of footsteps startled her for a brief moment. She tugged her wrapper closer and turned toward the figure emerging from the shadow of the pilot house. It was her father. He took only a few steps more before stopping.

"It looks as if neither of us could sleep," he said, his tone wary. "I would very much like to talk to you."

How strange that he should be almost asking permission to come to the rail with her. When she nodded, he walked closer, taking a position just out of her reach. He didn't look at her, but at the shore. His voice sounded older and broke a little with his first words. "I couldn't sleep because of my guilt," he said quietly, formally. "I have done you an injustice that I fear you might never forgive."

She turned, wishing his face was not hidden in shadow.

"I can only ask that you try to see my great error as a mistaken act of love."

His tone made her ache. "I know that," she said. "But it seems so cruel that you couldn't — "

He shook his head. "I'm not talking about what happened tonight, Gabrielle. My guilt is worse than that. When I wrote to invite David Wesley to travel with us, I hoped he would refuse. He did, as I told you. What I didn't tell you was that his mother's letter extended an invitation for you to come to visit at her home on land."

She gasped in disbelief.

"I know," he said, his tone dull. "But please try to imagine what was going through my mind. I was afraid, Gabrielle, afraid you would go to them, afraid you might choose that life over ours and be lost to me."

She stood silent and suddenly cold. What could she say to this that he didn't already know?

"I was sorry from the first day," he went on. "I saw your grief and it turned in me like a knife in a wound. I tried to think of something, anything, to make you happy. As much as I was afraid you would get hurt with that tightrope-walking act, I went along with it, hoping that might distract you from this other thing. I was wrong, Gabrielle. Now I don't even know how to ask your forgiveness."

Out in the woods he had talked about the tug-of-war within himself about her tightrope-walking, how he had feared it as a father, but praised it as a showman. Hers was a different tug-of-war. As a person she fiercely resented his interference in her life, his standing between her and the man she couldn't forget. As a daughter, she ached for him, knowing that he had only done this thing because he loved her so much.

"It may be too late to make amends," he said. "But tonight I made the only effort I could think of. I came to tell you earlier, but you were sleeping. I have written to Mrs. Wesley accepting her invitation for you to visit on her farm for a few days. Bony will take the letter to be posted in the morning."

Even if she had known what words to say, she could not have spoken them. Instead, she turned and flew against him, burying her head against his chest. He stroked her hair and then lifted her chin to look into her face. "I love you, my child."

Chapter
Eight

PRESENTING the same show for the second night in a single town along the river was not unheard of. But when the second performance of the *Levee Princess*'s new show, "Featuring Mademoiselle Gabrielle in her Death-Defying Rope Walk," still left as many eager show customers on the beach as had been fitted into the boat's auditorium, Gabrielle's father had no choice. He kept the boat tied up at the town dock for a third night to repeat the show again.

Stephen DuBois had been the world's worst pest before the night of Gabrielle's first performance. From that night on he avoided both her and her acts. Even at meals he was careful to sit where their eyes wouldn't meet. But, then, Gabrielle thought with wicked satisfaction, he didn't look at much of anything that first day after his fight with David Wesley on the gangplank. His right eye, which had only been swollen that evening, turned a fierce dark blue ringed by ugly yellow. Was it possible that he was afraid she might mention that her "mama's boy" had been enough of a man that it took three of the showboat crew to throw him off the boat?

But again she found herself restless with waiting. And so many questions spun in her head. Would Mrs. Wesley regret her invitation to have Gabrielle in her home, and not even answer her father's letter? She certainly had every right to be angry after not getting a prompt reply to her invitation, and then having her son so roughly treated by the men of the *Levee Princess*. Then there was the question she could hardly bear to ask herself: Did she really want to go even if the invitation was repeated?

Flossie acted strangely when Gabrielle tried to talk about visiting David and his mother. "You know the woman as well as I do," Flossie reminded her. "How can I give you advice about going to her home?"

"You said she was excitable," Gabrielle reminded her. "Surely she wouldn't have asked me if she didn't want to give me a fair chance."

Flossie raised her delicate eyebrows and lowered them again without comment.

But the other members of the staff who hadn't even met Mrs. Wesley treated Gabrielle strangely, too, after Bony took her father's letter off to town. One by one each of them had come to Gabrielle privately with praise and congratulations on her new act. But their manner was different. Instead of treating her as one of the close-knit circle of the cast, they acted almost as if she had become an outsider, as if she had ceased to be a showboat person merely by planning to make a brief visit on land.

Only her father seemed unchanged, warm, loving, and jovial whenever she was with him. After the parade on the third day she looked for him on the shady side of the deck where he usually sat reading. When he wasn't there, she went to the pilot house. He was sitting at his desk which was buried under blueprints and drawings of the newer, bigger boat he had always dreamed of having built. Gabrielle had heard its dimensions so many times she knew them by heart. She knew what color he wanted the curtain to be, a grand curtain that would be weighted to pull shut between acts.

She approached her father and put her arm across his shoulder. He hastily folded the plans and turned toward her.

"Thinking about starting the *Levee Queen?*" she asked. He had long ago chosen that grander name for the new craft.

"Heavens no," he said. "You know how I fool around with these blueprints whenever I have idle time."

She perched on the edge of his bunk and grinned at him. "On a hot day like this with the only breeze out there on deck? My guess is that the full house the last few days has given you hope that you will finally have enough money to get the boat built."

He nodded. "The money has been good here, I can't deny it. But I'm not making any plans."

The meaning behind his words struck her with a shock. How could he make plans? It was no secret that her new act was what would bring in the extra crowds — and the money along with them. Once she was gone, there would be no new act or extra money. "Father," she breathed, "I hadn't even thought of what it would do to the show if I left for almost a week. How will you manage?"

"Here," he said, turning to pat her hand lightly. "None of that. Sure, we'll have to shift things around a little, but that's no problem. If — *when* you hear from the Wesleys, you are not to give it a second thought."

She glanced at the half-covered blueprints. "Tell me true. If we kept making extra money like this, could you afford to have the boat built when we reach the Louisiana bayous for Christmas time?"

"I'm a magician, not a fortune-teller." He laughed and rose. "Let's go up on deck and take in a little of that cool breeze you were telling me about."

"I've never seen you get those plans out except when the money was coming in well," she told him, rising to follow.

It was cooler on deck. Gabrielle dozed in a chair, listening to her father and Judd Harper talk about the election coming up in the fall. Women in Wyoming had the right to vote. Maybe, she reflected, if she could vote, too, she would care more about who was going to be President.

Just as they were getting up to go down to the dining room for dinner, a half-grown boy came running down the path to the beach. His face was hidden under a ragged wide-brimmed straw hat as he came to the end of the dock and shouted for "the captain."

Gabrielle gathered with the others at the rail and heard the boy shout, "Message for Captain Prentice."

"The rest of you go on below and start dinner," her father said. "I'll be along when I see what this is about."

Gabrielle didn't move. Maybe she was more fortune-teller than magician. She knew as her father handed the boy a coin and took the envelope that the reply had finally come from Mrs. Wesley. She pressed the palms of her hands together tightly to stop her trembling.

Her father's face was expressionless as he slit the envelope, read the contents, then handed the letter to Gabrielle:

My Dear Captain Joshua Prentice,
Your letter received. We will be
gratified to welcome your daughter
as a guest in our home. With your

*permission, my son and I will attend
this evening's performance. I have
obtained local rooms in the home
of Mistress Barnes, a widow lady
held in high regard. It seems
reasonable that Miss Gabrielle could
return here with us tonight to
Mistress Barnes' house with a view
to our starting back to our home
early tomorrow.*

*If this plan proves not to be
acceptable, we could discuss other
arrangements this evening after the
performance.*

*With good wishes,
Bertha H. Wesley*

Underneath she had written:
Mrs. Benjamin R. Wesley

Gabrielle looked up at her father.

"Do you find the arrangements acceptable?" he asked.

"Yes, but — " she began.

"You might need more time to prepare
yourself, to pack clothing," he suggested.

She shook her head. "It's not that, Father.
I'm scared to death. If I put it off one minute, I'll never have the nerve." More than
anything she wanted him to tell her she didn't
have to accept at all. He didn't. He only
waited.

"What does that last line mean?" she
asked.

"I'd guess it was just the lady's way of telling us what her husband's name is."

"David never mentioned his father to me."

"Maybe you and David haven't had enough time together to do much talking. How long did you figure to stay?"

When she shook her head helplessly, he took the letter and folded it into his pocket. "I had suggested to Mrs. Wesley I could spare you almost a week. If that sounds fair to you, I could send a buggy up to bring you back down to the boat next Sunday."

"Father," she cried, not really knowing what she wanted to say.

He waited a minute, then put his arm around her shoulder. "You don't have to make up your mind this moment. Think about it through dinner and dressing. I'm sure Flossie will help you get your things together." He steered her toward the passageway, which rang with the clatter of serving dishes and the cheerful voices of the rest of the cast starting their afternoon meal.

Tom Luce had caught an immense catfish which Flossie had baked in a breading of browned buttered crumbs. Tom stood up to fillet the fish, expertly laying back the fine white flesh on the plate Flossie held for him. Gabrielle let herself be served the fish along with a helping of tiny red potatoes whose skins had burst to let in the melted butter. She kept her eyes on her plate and tried to make the food go down past the lump of terror in her throat.

"Message from the governor?" Judd Harper teased. "Are he and his missus driving over from Jeff City to come to our shindig tonight? The way people are coming out from under logs to see our lady here, I wouldn't be surprised."

Gabrielle looked up to see her father's eyes on her. She knew he expected her to take this chance to tell the rest of the cast about her plans, but she wasn't sure she could get the words out.

"Close to that," her father finally said. "Gabrielle's friend from upriver is escorting his mother to the show tonight." When he paused, Gabrielle forced herself to speak in a voice she barely recognized.

"Then afterward," she said carefully, "I am going back to their home with them for a brief visit."

Bony's fork fell, striking a musical note from his plate. He stared at Gabrielle, his eyes wide with disbelief. "Whatever for?" When no answer came, he turned to the captain. "What sort of folderol is this? Who ever heard of a showboat person going to stay on land except when they were in jail?"

"Bony," Flossie said softly, "it's a visit and it's the captain's business."

"Of course it's the captain's business," Lance said sullenly. "But a cast member doesn't just go off during season for no cause. What about the show?"

"Hold up there, all of you," Judd Harper said quietly. "We did shows on this river when Gabrielle there couldn't yet stand on her feet and walk. We can do them again."

Gabrielle knew that only kindness lay behind Judd's words. If she hadn't been sure of that, she could have read it in the warm expression on his face. But Judd couldn't know how it hurt to have him almost say that they had gotten along without her before, they could do it again.

Pud Swallow leaned to touch her hand. "You just go and have a nice time, Gabrielle. Aside from missing you like sun on a cloudy day, we'll just get along fine."

Any other time a babble of questions would have boiled around the table. Captain Prentice's silence stopped all that. After a quiet, uncomfortable moment, Flossie cried, "Glory!" and leaped to her feet to run for the kitchen. "I forgot about those peach pies in the oven," she called back from the door. "Come along, Gabrielle, help me serve them up before they burn to a crisp."

Out of sight of the table, Flossie hugged Gabrielle close. "Don't you worry about your packing, lovie, I've got that all thought out. And don't be scared. That woman is going to end up proud to have you a guest in her house."

Gabrielle clung to her until Flossie pulled loose and thrust a stack of pie plates into her hands.

Flossie was as good as her word. By a little after five, she had filled a humpbacked leather trunk with wrappers, night dresses, pantaloons, petticoats, and freshly ironed dresses.

"But I'm not even staying a whole week," Gabrielle protested.

"There's no river breeze on land," Flossie reminded her. "I don't want that woman saying you aren't the cleanest, freshest-dressed girl that ever sat at her table."

On the very top, Flossie placed her own favorite apron, a white percale with a ruffle all around the hem and a wonderful butterfly sash in back. "But that's your dress-up apron," Gabrielle cried.

"It's only mannerly that you help your hostess with her work," Flossie told her. "And I'll not have that woman saying you're not the handiest little thing in the kitchen she ever saw, either."

Gabrielle, on her knees in front of the trunk, looked up in dismay. "Why am I doing this, Flossie?"

"That's for you to ask and your own heart to answer," Flossie said sharply.

"You don't think I should go," Gabrielle said.

Flossie let herself down to sit on the floor beside Gabrielle. Her eyes shone with tears and her voice was vibrant with fury. "What I think doesn't matter. What I know is that if that woman treats you harshly or makes your days miserable up there, I am going straight to a voodoo woman the day we hit New Orleans and have such a spell for hives put on her that she'll never stop scratching in this life."

Gabrielle stared at her, struck by the vivid image of Mrs. Wesley fighting a good, itchy case of hives. Suddenly they were both laughing helplessly with just the slightest hint of hysteria mixed in.

Gabrielle and her father watched from the Texas deck for Mrs. Wesley and David to appear in the crowd that gathered on the beach. Gabrielle saw them first. Mrs. Wesley was wearing a high-necked navy dress and bonnet in spite of the heat. David, his fair hair gleaming, wore a jacket over dark trousers and was even more handsome than she remembered. When Gabrielle tugged her father's sleeve to signal their appearance, he gestured for the gangplank to be let down. Offering her his arm, he led her down to the beach.

Her father nodded to the chorus of greetings that accompanied their passing. "Evening, Captain!" "Good to see you stayed over." "Been waiting three days now to see this new show!"

As always, Gabrielle felt a deep, tender pride as her father greeted one family after another by name with unfailing charm. Then they were facing Mrs. Wesley and David.

The captain bowed gallantly over Mrs. Wesley's offered hand. "Delighted to greet you," he told her before turning solemnly to shake hands with David. "I believe you have both met my daughter Gabrielle."

Gabrielle was grateful that she only had to curtsy without touching Mrs. Wesley's hand. As she looked up into David's face, she caught her breath sharply, suddenly glad she hadn't had a chance to say anything to Stephen DuBois about his black eye. David's rich suntan couldn't hide the deep bruise on his cheek around a fresh cut just healing.

Gabrielle watched her father bow slightly to offer Mrs. Wesley his arm. "Come, Madame," he said. "I am delighted to escort you aboard the *Levee Princess* as our guest."

Mrs. Wesley paused, her eyes wide, before accepting the captain's arm and walking stiffly by his side. "This is all an act," Gabrielle told herself furiously as the crowd parted to let them pass, the captain and Mrs. Wesley first, with her following, her hand lightly on David's arm.

Bony had tied a rope across the end of the gangplank. He took it away for them to pass, and only when they had gone on into the auditorium did she hear his familiar patter as he took money for the performance and welcomed the customers aboard.

Gabrielle and her father stayed with the Wesleys until time for the show to begin. As if they had been prompted (which they might have been for all Gabrielle knew) almost every member of the cast joined them to be introduced: Flossie and her husband, Lance;

Judd Harper; Tom Luce; as well as Pud Swallow.

Stephen DuBois was conspicuous by his absence.

As the charade went on, Gabrielle fought against her rising anger. This was like a burlesque of a bad play! Everything was overdone and overstated. For once Lance wasn't the worst offender. Mrs. Wesley managed to be even more sickening than he was. Butter wouldn't have melted in her mouth. Everything about the boat was "lovely," and she was gratified to be able to see "this talented young lady" perform before having the "great delight" of having her as a guest in her home.

In a way all that make-believe foolishness helped Gabrielle get through the evening. Her anger sustained her. How many rivers did they travel in a year? How many hundreds of people paid to sit in those seats and found joy and magic there? Yet Mrs. Wesley, who had talked so cruelly about show people, was getting the queen's treatment for free and didn't even know the difference!

Conscious of David's adoring eyes, his mother's unchanging face, and Stephen's glowering fury, she went through the most exhausting performance of her life.

Excitement rippled through the room when she opened her tiny parasol and stepped onto the rope for her act. She had never performed better and she knew it. Bony's sensitive rendition of the lovely old song became a part of her body, feeding into the very soles of her feet to keep the rhythm perfect. When she was at the top of the rope, turning to look down, she made the mistake of glancing at David's mother's face.

Mrs. Wesley was not even enjoying what she saw. In Gabrielle's mind, she was reacting with those awful words she had said to Gabrielle and Flossie that day in the ice-cream parlor. Her face was stiff with indignation. In that moment, Gabrielle knew for certain that her visit to the Wesleys was a terrible mistake. It was a mistake even to try to make peace with that woman. Then she met David's eyes, tender and filled with wonder. She bowed deeply once, and then again before running in breathless relief down the rope into her father's arms.

Captain Prentice insisted on escorting them all back to Mistress Barnes' house, with Gabrielle's trunk following between two eager young boys. After a cup of watery tea in the flustered widow's parlor, Gabrielle told her father good-bye.

He pressed a small package into her hand. "This is a little gift for your hostess," he told her quietly. She recognized the shape of the box. The box contained a replica of a tiny banjo carved in ivory with the strings and the details finished in scrimshaw. He had these made as gifts for mayors and notables who honored his boat with their presence. "And this is in case you need it," he added, handing her a small, heavy bag that she knew contained gold coins.

Then he was gone and she stood alone in a strange white room with an angled ceiling, standing beside a high brass bed covered with a knobby white spread.

She had never been so lonely in her entire life.

Chapter Nine

As usual, Gabrielle wakened before dawn.
She had slept only fitfully in Mistress
Barnes' soft brass bed. The *Levee Princess*
creaked and rattled and rocked all the time
against the incessant pressure of the river's
movement. The Barnes house not only stayed
perfectly still, but it was also eerily silent. If
that weren't enough, the room was stuffy and
hot. The breeze that almost always fanned
along the river after sundown did not reach
the tree-lined brick street where Mistress
Barnes lived.

With the coming of the first pale ribbons
of dawn, the silence at least was dispersed.
Gabrielle could not have gone back to sleep if
she had wanted to. The birds didn't even wait
for the sun to come up before beginning to
argue and squawk in the trees outside her
window. A horse and cart clattered along in

front of the house with dogs following, barking frantically.

Was it too late to change her mind? Did she dare to tell Mrs. Wesley that she had made a mistake in accepting her invitation? Mrs. Wesley had plainly hinted that the trip downriver had already caused an interruption in a busy season at her farm. Surely having a stranger in her house would only waste more valuable time.

Gabrielle sat up abruptly. Mrs. Wesley . . . Mrs. Wesley . . . Mrs. Wesley. . . . That woman was all she thought about. It was David she was coming to see, not his mother. And David wanted her there. Why was she giving his mother the satisfaction of almost driving her away from David?

And she had no doubts at all when she was actually with David. Her doubts even disappeared at the thought of him. She had felt a strange plunging feeling every time her eyes had met his during the evening just past.

"I have to go through with it," she whispered aloud to herself. "If I don't go now, I will never have a chance to get to know him. I will never know if I really love him." She couldn't bear going on just thinking about him all the time without even knowing why he affected her this way. He was so sure about love at first sight, but she didn't know that much about love. Yet what, besides being in love with him, would make her heart thump strangely and change her breathing when he was around?

The pitcher on the washstand had been filled the night before. The water was warm from the hot room. This made it pleasant to wash with, but impossible to drink. Long before she heard the first sounds from the household below, she was dressed and ready for the day, with her face washed and her hair carefully arranged with a ribbon that matched the deep green dress she had chosen to travel in.

David had already hitched the horse to the buggy when Gabrielle came down for breakfast. As always, his smile of greeting wiped away all doubt for a wonderful moment.

Mrs. Barnes had set the table with a bewildering number of small dishes. A white pitcher filled with fresh nasturtiums decorated the center of the table. David was wonderfully gallant, seating both of the older women before holding Gabrielle's chair. His mother's expression brought Gabrielle's doubt back in a painful rush. Between Mrs. Wesley's eagle eyes and David's tender glances every minute he thought she was looking away, Gabrielle found it hard to swallow her breakfast. She was greatly relieved when Mrs. Wesley rose, counted out a number of coins to their hostess, and declared it was time to start home.

The horse, its flesh gleaming with sweat, trotted along briskly under David's reins as he drove out of town and into the countryside. Mrs. Wesley, beside Gabrielle in the backseat of the buggy, rode mostly in silence, leaving Gabrielle free to study the passing scenery. It was wonderful to be so near the things she usually only saw fleetingly from the river: woods, fruit orchards fragrant with ripening fruit, and now and then a farmhouse flanked by barns and stables.

Wild flowers bloomed along the fence rows: blue asters, clumps of black-eyed daisies, and Queen Anne's lace that looked like tiny white bridal bouquets. Gabrielle thought nothing could be more satisfying than to be able to walk out the door and pick fresh flowers for your table!

The livestock in the fields were the most astonishing. The animals who came to water at the river's edge were mostly small: raccoons trailed by their young, sharp-nosed opossums, and boldly marked skunks who swaggered under their plumed tails. Once in a while deer came to the river's edge, but even they seemed delicate and fragile compared to the cattle and horses in the fields they passed. The hogs rooting in a muddy stream bed were bigger and more solid than they looked from the rail of a boat. When they passed a flock of dirty white sheep with black heads, Gabrielle leaned to stare at them with astonishment.

"A different world, isn't it?" Mrs. Wesley asked.

"Indeed it is," Gabrielle agreed. "The animals are so big."

From his seat in front, David laughed softly.

"Surely you ride horseback," Mrs. Wesley said.

Gabrielle shook her head. "I have had no reason to learn."

Mrs. Wesley's lips closed in a thin line and she fell silent again.

At noon they stopped at the edge of a grove. Mrs. Wesley spread out a checked tablecloth and unpacked a picnic of ham sandwiches, purple plums, and a tin of ginger cookies. When David finished unhitching the horse to lead it off into the woods for water, his mother seated herself stiffly on a fallen tree trunk and fixed Gabrielle with a solemn stare.

"This is a good time for us to talk," she said. "I didn't want to embarrass David by talking to you about him in his presence, but there are some things you need to understand. David Wesley is not just an ordinary young man. He was born and has been raised to be a respected member of our community. I was a Harper, you know, one of the pioneer families in Pike County. The Harpers have a position to maintain."

Gabrielle waited, not knowing how to respond to this. How little she really knew about David! Mrs. Wesley stared off into the trees as if gathering her thoughts.

"I can't think of any way to tell you this, except to say it right out straight. We Harpers don't let ourselves be puffed up by our position, but neither can we afford scandal. You must realize that for a Harper to entertain a show person is . . . highly irregular, if not unheard of."

Gabrielle dropped her eyes, fearful that Mrs. Wesley would see her rising annoyance. Why had this woman asked her to visit if she felt so much above her?

"In deference to the family reputation, you are not to mention to anyone that you are just a show girl. I think it's little to ask considering you are my guest and how severe the consequences would be."

Gabrielle tightened her hands in her lap. There was no shame in working as a show girl, but she wasn't "just a show girl." She was an actress and a singer. She even played the banjo and was studying the dulcimer with Flossie's help whenever she had time. How many times had people told her she was talented? Now, instead of taking pride in her work, she was suddenly expected to be ashamed of it.

Gabrielle heard David coming through the trees, talking quietly to his horse. Mrs. Wesley spoke again, quickly, her voice firm and a little threatening. "We *do* understand each other on this, don't we, Miss Prentice?"

Gabrielle nodded and murmured, "Yes, ma'am."

That, at least, was the truth. She understood entirely too well. The woman was not only a snob about her hateful Harper name, but she was also willing to do the same as lie to her friends about her guest.

Then David was smiling at her from the edge of the clearing and she remembered with a dazzling rush of excitement why she was putting herself through all this.

The drive went on forever. Gabrielle was conscious of the river to the east of them, hidden by groves of trees. Once in a while she heard the muffled signaling of a boat whistle and smelled the spicy scent of the mint that grew along the shore.

It was nearing dusk when David guided the horse onto a lane that wound off the country road up to the Wesley house. Once a line of huge trees had lined the lane, but here and there one had died, leaving giant dead limbs stark against the fading red of sunset. The house was two stories and square, set in a windbreak of cottonwood trees. Two large barns and a stable were off to the left near a smaller house whose chimney sent a pale thread of smoke up into the still air. A pair of horses cantered over to the fence to watch them approach, and a black dog leaped off the porch to greet them, his tail wagging wildly.

"Home," Mrs. Wesley said with satisfaction.

"It's lovely," Gabrielle said as David handed her down from the buggy. "Those wonderful wide porches." The dog circled them, whining and nosing at David.

"Grandpa Harper built it," Mrs. Wesley told her. "A fine man, my grandpa, a pillar in the community, the picture of my David here."

At his mother's disapproving glance, David released Gabrielle's hand and turned to lift her trunk and his mother's Gladstone bag from the storage area at the rear of the buggy.

The hall was so dark that Gabrielle couldn't see anyone at first. As her eyes adjusted, she saw a very small, older woman smiling up at her as David set down her trunk. Without waiting for an introduction, she reached out and took both of Gabrielle's hands.

"So this is our guest," she said in a warm tone. "You're every bit as pretty as David said you were. Welcome, my dear, welcome." Her hair was completely white above a square, tanned face webbed with tiny wrinkles. She was not even as tall as Gabrielle, but her slender back was as straight as if she, too, were sixteen. Gabrielle clung to her hands a moment, feeling a rush of happiness at the warmth of the old woman's welcome.

Mrs. Wesley broke in, her voice stiff with disapproval. "This is my mother. Mrs. Harper, Miss Prentice."

"Grandma Harper," the old woman corrected her. "I'm not much for those formalities. Come in, come in. The supper's cold but it's a-plenty."

The kitchen amazed Gabrielle. A great black range dominated one wall of the huge room. The round oak table stood on a fancy three-legged pedestal, and along another wall hung more kinds of pots and pans and cooking utensils than Gabrielle had ever even seen in a store.

Grandma Harper's description had been exactly right. The supper was cold but ample, more of the ham sliced on a platter with side dishes of cottage cheese, corn relish from Mrs. Wesley's garden, and homemade applesauce without nearly as much cinnamon as Flossie put in hers. Two luscious-looking pies with golden crusts waited on a shelf by the stove. David devoured the meal with obvious hunger, but Gabrielle, conscious of his eyes on her, again had trouble eating.

"You have a beautiful name," Grandma Harper said. "It's French, isn't it?"

Gabrielle nodded. "My mother was French."

"Then she must have taught you the language."

Gabrielle shook her head. "I was only tiny when she died of yellow fever. But the woman who cared for me was French, too, so I manage fairly well when we are in Cajun country."

The old woman's eyes sparkled with delight. "What a wonderful accomplishment. Tell me — "

"Mother," Mrs. Wesley interrupted her. "Miss Prentice must be exhausted. We were up very late last night and got an early start this morning. I am sure Miss Prentice wants nothing more than a pitcher of hot water to freshen up with and a good night's rest."

"But, Mother," David protested, "it's not even eight o'clock. I wanted to show Gabrielle around the place."

"Don't be so stuffy, Bertha," her mother snapped. "Of course the young people want to walk out together. They need to stretch their legs. They've been cooped inside a dusty buggy all day."

Mrs. Wesley hesitated a long moment before sighing. "Very well, David, if you must, although I can't imagine what you think you can see in the dark. But no loitering anywhere. We were *all* up late last night."

A slender paring of moon hung in a sky crowded with stars. In among the line of trees that edged the road, the lightning bugs winked back and forth like pale green torches. David took Gabrielle's hand the moment they were out of sight of the porch. Once in the shadow of the walnut tree between the house and the barn fence, he seized her and pulled her into his arms, searching for her lips with his own. "I can't believe this," he said. "I can't believe I actually have you here!"

"David," she whispered, turning her head away, "what are you doing? Let me go."

He only held her closer, shaking his head. "Don't you know I have been dying to do this all day, every day, since I first saw you?

Surely you feel the same or you wouldn't have come here."

"That's not true at all," she said, flattening her hands on his chest to break free of his grip. "I came because I wanted to get to know you better. That's all."

He pulled back and looked at her. "My, how prim we sound! But if that's the way you want it, that's how it will be." He laughed genially and took her hand and tucked it under his arm. "All girls talk like that, but nobody ever believes them. But never mind. You're here, that's all that matters."

The black dog panted along behind them, stopping once in a while to nose at a shrub or inspect a fence post. As they went by the barn lot, a sharp, acrid scent made Gabrielle's eyes sting. She held her breath until they were past it. From inside the barn she heard the horses stamping, and from somewhere beyond, the fretful clucking of chickens.

A light appeared suddenly in the distance as a lamp was lit in the smaller house beyond the second barn. "Who lives there?" she asked.

"Jim and Daisie Keeler," he told her. "Jim's our hired man, and his wife, Daisie, keeps house for Mother and helps with the gardening and canning."

"Your mother is a widow?"

He tightened his grip on her arm. "I don't even remember my father. He left when I was only a little kid." He turned suddenly, taking her shoulders in his hands. "I don't want to talk about that, Gabrielle. I don't want to talk about anything but us. Tell me that you love me the way I love you."

"Don't ask me to say something I can't say, David. I think about you a lot and I love being with you, but how can I know about love so soon?"

"Soon!" he cried. "I knew the moment I saw you there, poised like a butterfly up in the air."

"Butterfly," she teased him. "Believe me, there's more to me than any butterfly."

He laughed and gripped her suddenly by the waist, lifting her above his head. Startled, she clutched at him. He let her down into his arms until their faces were very close together. "I love you, Gabrielle," he whispered. "I've never loved any girl like this before, never in my life. I go to bed thinking about you, and wake up the same way. Tell me you won't ever leave me. Tell me you'll stay here with me forever."

"I can't do that," she protested. "Now please put me down and be sensible. Don't spoil our time together by suggesting impossible things. Come next Sunday my father will send a buggy for me and I will go back home."

He set her lightly on the ground and smiled down at her. "Maybe he will and maybe he won't. In any case, by then we'll have our plans all made for you to come back for good."

Gabrielle stared at him. "David," she said,

"quit that! Don't you understand? I just came for a visit."

He shrugged. "All right, we won't argue about it now. But I have to warn you that I almost always get my way."

"So do I," she told him, pulling her hand free to walk away. They walked only a few minutes apart before reaching the shadow of the barn. David caught her hand again, his voice low and appealing. "Please, Gabrielle, just let me hold you a minute. I have waited so long."

Touched by his tone, she let him draw her into his arms. Without warning he tightened his grip and lifted her chin so that their lips touched. His mouth was warm and soft against hers. The strangest kind of excitement froze her there for a long moment. When she finally pulled away, he was smiling down at her. "I love you, Gabrielle," he said softly and reached out for her again.

"No, David," she said firmly, turning to walk away.

"Now don't try to tell me you didn't like being kissed," he said, catching up with her. "I don't know why girls always pretend they don't want to be kissed. It's only natural for them to like it as much as boys — men — do."

"I'm tired of your telling me what girls like and don't like," she said, walking a little faster. "Maybe I'm different from all the other girls you have known."

"You are, Gabrielle," he said softly, taking

her arm. "That's why I love you so very, very much."

She sighed. Why did she blow hot and cold like this? One moment he irritated her so much she wanted to strike out at him. Then his voice turned soft like that and she wanted to throw herself in his arms and comfort him. He must have sensed her feelings because his arm was around her again in a flash.

"That's that," she said, pulling away. "I simply will not be treated like this, David. If you think I'm not a lady just because I am an actress and singer, you have a great deal to learn. Unless you want me to turn right around and go back home, you have to quit grabbing and tugging at me all the time."

For the first time she heard a hint of anger in his voice. "If you didn't want to be with me, why did you come?"

A lantern appeared at the front door and Mrs. Wesley, the planes of her face exaggerated by the half light, called his name. "We're right here, Mother," he said quickly.

For once Gabrielle was actually glad to see the woman. She didn't have any answer to David's question that she could put into words.

"The farm is lovely," she told Mrs. Wesley, following her into the hall.

Her hostess nodded with an air of satisfaction. "This place is famous all over the county. Wait until you see it in full sun."

The pride in Mrs. Wesley's voice reminded Gabrielle of her father's feeling about the *Levee Princess*. The big difference was that when anyone said such nice things about his showboat, her father had the grace to say, "Thank you."

Chapter Ten

GABRIELLE had never thought of the schedule on the *Levee Princess* as being particularly easy and graceful. Everyone worked, most of them at two jobs or more, but she never felt pushed. It was as if the workdays flowed with the simple rhythm of the river that bore the boat along. She was not at all prepared for the harried schedule of the Wesley household.

While it was true that none of the humans on the farm got up as early as three in the morning, the animals didn't miss it by much.

Before the first glint of dawn, a huge bronze-colored rooster flapped up onto a fence post and began crowing as if he were paid by the squawk. The hens came spilling out of the chicken coop to cluck and squabble. Not long after that the cows began to bellow to be milked. This wakened the black dog, whose name was Nappie. His steady barking roused other dogs all over the area. This chorus of yapping even managed to drown out the constant twittering of the songbirds outside Gabrielle's window.

But the animals ran the people on a farm, anyway, Gabrielle decided. From her window she saw David going through the gate toward the barn before she had finished dressing. As she finished making her bed, she heard the clatter of his return. He was whistling and swinging two full milk pails, a cluster of spotted kittens running along behind him. He had no sooner disappeared into the house before his mother came out and started for the chicken coop with a basket of grain. Gabrielle pulled back as Mrs. Wesley glanced toward her window, embarrassed at being caught watching.

Grandma Harper was alone in the kitchen when Gabrielle entered. "Look who's here!" the old woman said with a smile. "What's got you up so bright and early?"

The line of poetry came to Gabrielle's mind automatically: "The cock, that is the trumpet of the morn."

Grandma Harper put down the plate she was carrying and stared at her. "I recognize that line," she said. "That's Shakespeare. My goodness, child, you do have some learning! But then I guess with the plays — "

Mrs. Wesley stopped her from the door. "Mother," she said sternly, "have you already forgotten what I said?"

"Sorry," her mother said tartly. "I was carried away by having the joy of hearing *Hamlet* quoted before breakfast."

"Good morning, Mrs. Wesley," Gabrielle said. "Have you a job for me? I'd be happy to help."

Mrs. Wesley dismissed her offer with a shrug. "Daisie will be along any minute now. That's what we pay her for. You just stay out of everyone's way and we'll all be fine."

Grandma Harper glared at her daughter. "What a way to talk to this child! Come along with me, Gabrielle. I want to show you my private garden."

Before Grandma Harper wiped her hands to join Gabrielle, Daisie Keeler came in through the back door, wearing a ragged calico apron. She was a round-faced young woman with a generous spattering of freckles across her button nose. She looked away and mumbled a shy greeting when Gabrielle was introduced.

Outside, Grandma Harper took Gabrielle's arm and looked up at her with a look of mischief. "You don't have to look at my garden unless you want to. I just wanted to get you out of range of my daughter's tongue. If you judge a mother by her daughter's manners, I'm not much of a success. But I take no blame in her case. Her father spoiled her as badly as she is spoiling that David of hers."

Gabrielle was almost too astonished by the woman's frankness to make any reply. "I'd really love to see your garden," she finally stammered.

Grandma Harper laughed. "I should have warned you that I'm not much for polite social lies."

"Neither am I," Gabrielle admitted.

The old woman paused and studied Gabrielle thoughtfully. "Then why in tarnation did you agree to keep it a secret where you came from?"

"I didn't really agree," Gabrielle told her. "Your daughter said that's what I had to do, and I said I would."

Grandma Harper sniffed. "You'd think she would have learned by now that the truth always comes out in the end, in spite of all."

The outside air was alive with sound. Bees hummed in the honeysuckle climbing against the side of the chicken coop, and a pair of crows rose screeching from a tree at the back of what looked like a huge family garden. Dead corn stalks, sagging tomato vines, and the ruins of bean rows ran the length of the huge fenced lot. Only the pumpkins and some crookneck squash still flourished among green leaves.

Grandma Harper's garden was only a small patch behind the larger garden. Grandma Harper peered at her own neat rows of bushes and asked Gabrielle if she knew what they were.

Gabrielle kneeled. "This looks like the rosemary that Flossie uses when she cooks chicken."

"Very good," the old woman nodded. "The next one is sage, and then summer savory. Catch a handful of that big, untidy bush with the flowers on it at the end and see what it smells like."

"Oh," Gabrielle sighed, crushing the silvery leaves in her hand. "How beautiful and fresh. What is it?"

"Lavender. I dry it and put it with clothes and linen. I'll fix some of it for you if you'd like."

As Gabrielle smiled and rose, the old woman touched her arm as if she were pleading. "Don't let Bertha's sharp tongue drive you off. She's been bitter ever since David's father walked off and left her. She acts like that because she's afraid."

"Afraid?" Gabrielle asked. What possible harm could she do to the strong, forceful Mrs. Wesley?

"Because of David," the older woman went on. "He's all she has now. But David needs someone with spunk like you. It would be the making of him."

"Did I hear my name being mentioned?" David asked, coming down the row along the garden. His eyes were bright on Gabrielle, and that wonderful smile was like a second sun. The fine sheen of sweat on his face made his skin glow like polished metal.

"Eavesdroppers never hear good of themselves," his grandmother said, taking his arm. "I must say, though, your little lady is all you said she was, plus a lot more."

The sudden angry clanging of the bell by the kitchen door drowned out her words. Gabrielle looked up to see Mrs. Wesley clinging to the rope, glaring at David. "What do you think you are doing out there? You know breakfast is on the table."

"I just wanted to say good morning to Gabrielle," he said, stepping past her to hold the door open.

"That's all very well for people of leisure. Jim is already out there harnessing the horses. There's hay to be brought in from the north forty today."

"Does it have to be done today?" he asked. "I wanted to take Gabrielle — "

Grandma Harper silenced him by laying her hand on his arm. "Come eat, David. The quicker into the field, the quicker out."

Grandma Harper went off to her room immediately after breakfast, but Mrs. Wesley flew from one job to the next all morning long. She checked the evil-smelling sauerkraut in the big gray jug with a weight on the top, and simmered milk for cottage cheese on the back of the stove. Then she filled a tall, thin, wooden tub with cream and turned to Gabrielle. "Do you know how to make butter?"

"I'm sure I can learn if you tell me how," she said.

Mrs. Wesley shook her head and sat on a small stool to brace the churn between her knees. "Cream brings too much at the market to risk it being spoiled. Look around. Surely you can find *some* way to amuse yourself."

Gabrielle, simmering with resentment, was glad to escape. She couldn't believe any woman worked like that all the time. She was only showing off to make Gabrielle feel stupid and helpless. Gabrielle wandered out to the barn to look for the kittens, but the smell of the barnyard drove her away before she could lure one to her hand.

She leaned for a while, watching the chickens scratch and chase each other. Everything was dusty — the fence she had leaned on, even the feathers of the poultry. The sun was hot and high over her head, and when she looked across the pasture, heat shimmered in the air, distorting the shapes of the distant trees.

With the sun like that it must be nearing noon. The cast of the *Levee Princess* would be coming back from the parade, carrying their band instruments. With a twinge of guilt, she thought about Flossie, who would have no one to help her with that big afternoon meal.

The trees beyond the pasture looked cool and green. She slipped under the fence to walk toward them. The grass was dusty and a cloud of grasshoppers leaped before her feet. A box turtle scrambled out of her path and closed itself into its shell when she leaned to look at it.

"I'm sick of animals, anyway," she told it, yearning for the river. She paused, wondering how far they were from its banks. She listened, hoping to hear the distant signaling of a boat horn. Instead, that hateful bell rang again and she knew it was time for lunch.

When she turned to go back to the house, she gasped. A large brown and white cow had come from nowhere to stand between her and the fence. The creature was immense, with one crooked horn and one straight one. She stared at Gabrielle steadily, her jaw working back and forth sideways as saliva foamed around her mouth.

"Go away," Gabrielle told her.

When the cow didn't move, Gabrielle started to cut a wide circle around her. The cow followed on swift hooves, and began bellowing at her. Panic-stricken, Gabrielle picked up her skirts and ran as fast as she could through the dry stubble of the field. She heard the big animal puffing along behind her, and gasped for breath. As she reached the fence and rolled under it, she heard a gale of laughter from the direction of the house.

David was running toward her, grinning from ear to ear. He caught her hand and pulled her to her feet. "Oh, Gabrielle," he said, fighting his laughter, "I should have warned you. That's Lily. She wouldn't hurt you. She was hand-raised and likes to make up to people."

Gabrielle, her heart pounding and her clothes streaked with dust, was not amused. "I hate her," she said hotly. "She chased me."

He gently drew her hand in under his arm. "Come on. How can you hate a dumb beast like a cow?"

"Easy," she said, still fighting for breath. "I hate all cows. And maybe horses, too. I'm not sure about that yet."

"David," his mother called from the porch. He dropped her hand as if it had suddenly burst into flame.

Since Daisie had carried a lunch to Jim in the field, there were only the four of them at the table. The fried chicken tasted wonderful until it occurred to Gabrielle that it had probably been scratching in the yard the day before.

"I was interested in what my mother said about your being educated," Mrs. Wesley said with a skeptical expression. "Then you must not have lived on that boat all your life."

"Oh, but I have," Gabrielle told her. "But Flossie made me do lessons every day when I was growing up."

"You mean that older actress was your only teacher?"

"Flossie was a teacher on land before she ran away and married her husband, Lance." The minute the words were out, Gabrielle regretted them.

David must have seen his mother's shocked expression because he spoke quickly. "I didn't recognize her in the play for a few minutes. She looked years older than I remembered."

"Makeup," Gabrielle explained. "It's wonderful, but it can only make you older, never younger."

Mrs. Wesley obviously didn't like talk about makeup any better than she had liked hearing about Flossie running away. Happily, Grandma Harper asked for more rhubarb pie and began telling Gabrielle a long story about her husband's favorite kinds of pies.

Gabrielle had never taken a nap in her life that she could remember except when she was sick. That afternoon she leaped on Grandma Harper's suggestion that a rest might feel good on such a hot afternoon. She went up to her room and closed the door as soon as David left for the field to join Jim Keeler.

To her own amazement, she slept. The afternoon was almost spent before she wakened and went downstairs. She had just joined Grandma Harper on the front porch when a buggy pulled in at the drive, bringing a Mrs. Forrester to call. She was a pleasant woman of Grandma Harper's age with fine, gray hair curiously tinged with pink. Mrs. Wesley brought out a glass pitcher of iced tea with sprigs of mint from her mother's herb garden, and a plate of wonderful cookies with a tart raisin filling. After serving these she concentrated wholly on keeping Gabrielle from saying the wrong things to their guest.

"I heard at the store that David had a

friend visiting," Mrs. Forrester said, her eyes friendly on Gabrielle. "Where did you say you were from, dear?"

"She was born in New Orleans, in Louisiana," Mrs. Wesley replied. "I am delighted to hear that you've been in town today. Tell me, is there any word yet about the Thompson baby? It must be due by now."

Mrs. Forrester looked a little surprised to have the subject changed so abruptly, but said she had heard nothing and turned again to Gabrielle. The conversation would have made a good comic show on the boat, but only if Gabrielle were a dummy and David's mother a ventriloquist. Everytime Mrs. Forrester asked a question of Gabrielle, Mrs. Wesley answered it and brought up some new subject. Grandma Harper kept rocking a little faster and a little faster, until Gabrielle expected her painted wicker rocker to take off and fly.

Finally Grandma Harper had had enough of what she must have known was terribly embarrassing to Gabrielle. "I see David coming through the pasture with the team," she said, interrupting her daughter. "I know he would love to have you bring him a nice glass of tea, Gabrielle."

Gabrielle leaped up, excused herself to Mrs. Forrester, and fled to fix the tea for David, pretending not to notice Mrs. Wesley's angry glare.

Gabrielle waited at the fence of the barn lot until David brought in the horses, slipped off their harnesses, and released them to go to the water trough. When he came to the fence he smiled as he reached for the tea. There it was again, that crazy excitement she always felt when she was with him.

"You don't know how beautiful you are, standing there waiting for me," he said, touching her hand as he took the glass. "That's all I've thought about all day, you know, just getting to come back to you."

He paused and cocked his head as if he were waiting. "Come on, aren't you even going to tell me you missed me?"

She nodded. "I did miss you. I really did."

"That's better," he said. Then he glanced at the three women on the porch. "If we didn't have such an audience, I'd welcome you properly."

"Ha!" she said. "You mean you would try to welcome me *improperly*."

He laughed softly. "Small difference of opinion there. After I clean up, maybe we could drive into town before supper."

"Maybe we could," she said, suddenly overwhelmed again with that crazy indecision she felt about David. Looking at him like this, seeing the tenderness in his eyes, and feeling that almost dangerous excitement, she knew that if no one had been watching and he hadn't been dripping from sweat from the field, she would have liked to lean against him and have him hold her close.

Maybe she would even like the feel of his lips on hers again.

She and David were not permitted to drive into town before supper. From the coolness between David and his mother during that meal, she guessed he had not given up easily. After helping her hostess straighten the kitchen, she was astonished to have David invite her for a buggy ride.

She didn't know and didn't care how he had talked his mother into letting the two of them out together, but she was pretty sure that Grandma Harper had had a hand in it. In any case, it was wonderful to get away from that house, and exciting to step up into the buggy with her shawl over her arm and set out in the cooling breeze of early evening.

David beamed with happiness as the horse cantered down the lane that led from the house. Just before he reached the road, he tugged the horse to a stop. "Now look through there," he said.

She leaned in the direction he pointed and gasped. The river. The last light of day shimmered on its moving face. As she looked, a dark shape, lit with high lanterns, moved slowly into view, then passed on downriver. A loaded barge on its way south — maybe zinc from the mines in northern Illinois or lumber from Hannibal, Missouri.

"I didn't realize you could see the river from your place."

"This is the only spot close to the house," he told her. "I'm surprised you didn't find it today."

"I will tomorrow," she promised as he loosened the reins and let the horse take the buggy on without direction.

"I wish I didn't have to work all the time while you're here," he told her. "But it is a busy season."

"Is there ever a time that isn't busy?" she asked.

He looked at her, puzzled.

"You know, all those animals," she said. "Don't they have to be fed and watered and milked and their eggs gathered all the time?"

He roared with laughter. "Sure, they do, but that's nothing. Work is when you have to get out in the field and sweat all day, like I did today. Work is what takes me away from you."

He took both reins in his left hand and slid his other arm around her shoulder. "Lean against me," he said. "You can put your head back and see the stars."

For the first few moments she felt stiff and fearful. If he was going to grab her as he had the night before, he was going to have a fight on his hands! Instead, he kept the horse moving and made no motion toward her. And he was right. The stars were crowded in the darkening sky and his shoulder felt warm and solid behind her.

"Tell me about the people on the boat," he said after a while.

"You met them all, I think," she said lazily. "My father and Flossie and Judd Harper. . . ." She went on with the list and he waited until she fell silent.

"There's got to be one more," he said. "The guy who busted me in the face when I tried to get on board that night. The wiry, dark guy with a fist like a rock."

"Oh," she said. "That's Stephen DuBois."

"What does he do on the boat?"

"He's a gymnast and a dancer and does some songs. He's very talented."

"Not to mention that he's in love with you."

She straightened in her seat to turn to stare at him. "Stephen? He hates me."

David reached over and pulled her head back down on his shoulder. "That may be what he tells you, but he was out to kill me that night."

"He'd kill for my father, maybe," Gabrielle said. "But he can't stand me."

"That's not the way I heard it."

Gabrielle fell silent. What had he heard? What had Stephen said about her to David that gave him such a crazy impression? She wanted to ask, but somehow didn't want to know.

But David went on, his voice thoughtful. "It's none of my business yet, Gabrielle, but isn't it kind of dangerous to have only you two women on board with all those men, and you're the only one with no husband to protect her?"

The thought of Lance protecting Flossie almost made her giggle. "It's not like that at all," she told him. "We're like a family. We all live together and work together and like each other. Except for Stephen," she added hastily, "who doesn't like me."

"Well, I don't like it, Gabrielle," he said softly. "A beautiful girl like you deserves a proper life with a nice home of her own."

"I have a proper life," she told him, feeling herself stiffening again.

He tied the reins beside him and reached to take her into his arms. "Listen to me," he whispered. "A proper life is to sleep in a solid house on land and have a husband who adores you. To have children — a girl with black hair like yours, and maybe a son or two. To wake up safe and loved every day, the way I love you."

When he was gentle this way, she didn't even want to pull away. He made that life sound so wonderful, almost like a dream, like the dream she had cherished as a child watching the land slip by as the *Levee Princess* traveled the rivers. How many times had she felt sorry for herself not to live like land people? Now he was offering it to her. But something in her heart held her back.

He cupped her face in his hands and tilted it up so he could see directly into her eyes. The moon glanced off his strong, well-shaped features, and his lips touched hers so gently that it seemed they belonged there.

She clung to him a long time, feeling her heart hammering against his chest. His mother was getting in the way. That's all it was. If there were just the two of them, David and herself, the dream could be real.

Then he sighed. "If we don't go back, we won't be let off that place together again all week. And Saturday night there's a barn dance I get to take you to!"

She rode with her head in the hollow of his shoulder all the way home.

Chapter
Eleven

Tɪᴍᴇ, which passed so swiftly on the *Levee
Princess*, slowed to a crawl during that week
on the Wesley farm. To Gabrielle, accustomed to the constantly changing scenery
along the river, the monotony of the land was
unbelievable. Every day she walked under
the same whispering trees and through the
stubble of dusty pastures humming with insects. Even the sun rising in a blaze of heat
seemed to toil across the sky with a dogged
persistence, like Mrs. Wesley brought to the
endless treadmill of her daily work.

She found that even when a change in the
routine promised possible excitement, the
result managed to bring her pain or unhappiness.

There was the morning that David hitched
a single horse to a flat-bed wagon and drove
his mother and Gabrielle to gather apples.

This was a part of the farm she hadn't seen before. The farther the wagon traveled from the farmhouse, the wilder and more interesting she found her surroundings. They passed through an endless series of wooden gates; past lines of ancient trees; and along a dry creek bed lined with smooth, silver-colored stones. Birds new to Gabrielle were everywhere, scarlet cardinals flashing and calling, quail skimming through the grass as if they had wheels. When the wagon finally stopped at a broken-down fence, brown rabbits bolted away in panic.

David had told her that the orchard was old, dating from Grandpa Harper's early days. Wild oats and matted weeds grew ragged and untended between the trees. Here and there rose clumps of wild flowers; chicory with blossoms the same clear blue color as the sky; clumps of giant clover with rounded, rosy heads as big as Gabrielle's thumbs; and the black-eyed daisies that David called "Susans." Everywhere red apples gleamed brightly from among green leaves, and a furious blue jay screamed angrily at the intrusion of humans.

Gabrielle slid to the ground and drew in a deep, delicious breath. The air smelled like cider from the windfall apples in the grass. David smiled as he pulled down a low branch to choose a perfect apple. After polishing it on his shirttail, he handed it to her. She had grown accustomed to his silence when his mother was with them. In a way, it was almost more romantic to try to read his thoughts as his hand brushed hers and he smiled into her eyes.

Mrs. Wesley made it clear at once that they were there for work, not "idle amusement."

David was allowed to climb the trees, but Gabrielle didn't dare ask if she could. She and Mrs. Wesley picked the fruit from the low branches, putting the perfect apples in one basket and the ones the birds had eaten from or which were overripe in another.

As they worked, Mrs. Wesley talked about what she did with this glowing harvest of apples. "We sell them, and make cider and sell that. We dry them, and bake them into pies." She glanced at a basket almost full of imperfect fruit. "And we cook those down into apple butter."

"Don't forget bobbing for them in tubs of water on Halloween," David called from the top of the tree above them.

Mrs. Wesley only mumbled and emptied her apronful of apples into the basket.

By the time the first brimming baskets of scarlet fruit were loaded into the wagon, Gabrielle had begun to itch. She glanced at her ankles in dismay. There were mosquitoes and willow beetles on the river, but she had never heard of a bug that could bite clear through a pair of cotton stockings. But something had to be getting her. She felt a sharp sting, then a burning that grew steadily worse with every minute. She yearned to scratch, but didn't dare. Not content with only her legs, the insects moved steadily up her body. When the itching and burning reached the tender flesh under her belt, she was desperate for relief. She watched the wagon being loaded with full baskets, hoping against hope that every one would be the last.

Since it wasn't any more ladylike to scratch than it was to spit or whistle, she tightened her lips together and suffered silently. The sun stood high in the sky, signaling noon, before Mrs. Wesley announced that they had picked enough to start back home.

The fragrance of Daisie's stew filled Gabrielle's senses as they entered the kitchen. "We'll clean up and be right down," Mrs. Wesley told her. "You might polish up a bowl of that fruit for the table."

Gabrielle fled to her room and pulled off her stockings to examine herself. It hadn't been her imagination! Tiny red spots dotted her ankles and the warm flesh on the back of her knees. A perfect band of spots circled her slender waist where her sash had held the fabric close to her skin. She sat on the edge of her bed near tears. Just insects couldn't have done all that! Maybe she had come down with a fever that just happened to break out while she was in the orchard. Maybe she was going to be dreadfully sick away from her father and Flossie and the river. Maybe she even had something she could give to the Wesley family and make them sick, too. At the thought, she slid her feet back into her shoes, tiptoed down the hall to Grandma Harper's room, and rapped on the door.

"Whatever is the matter, child?" Grandma Harper asked, looking in dismay at Gabrielle's face.

Gabrielle spilled out her fears in a tumble of words and raised her skirt to display the welts on her ankles. The old woman caught her in a hug.

"For heaven's sake, child, those are chiggers. Who would have thought you didn't know about chiggers? You get right back to your room and wash every one of those bites with heavy soapsuds and water. And don't put your clothes back on until I get there."

By the time Gabrielle finished washing, Grandma Harper had been downstairs and was back with a bowl of whitish powder.

The old woman chatted sympathetically as she moistened the bites with fresh water and dusted them with baking soda. "Missouri grass is thick with those little spiders, and they itch like thunder," she told Gabrielle. "There's no way to stop that burning except with soda. But don't worry. No harm comes from them unless you scratch up an infection."

"There," she said at last, dabbing the last of the bites and smiling up at Gabrielle. "You are one little lady," she said quietly. "Coming in here affire with chigger bites and only worrying that you might have some fever to pass on to us. I fault David for a lot of things, but he sure knew his business when he picked you. Now we better get downstairs. I told Bertha not to clang that blasted bell, that we'd be to lunch when we were full ready."

The rest of the family had almost finished eating. David's expression showed just enough amusement in it to make Gabrielle so furious that she wouldn't return his glance. She was relieved when Mrs. Wesley excused herself to have David set a fire for the apple butter before he left for the field work.

That afternoon nap was Gabrielle's own idea. She slept between sheets that Grandma Harper had generously dusted with soda.

She wakened to air scented with cinnamon and apple, and to the sound of voices wafting up from the shady porch. The apple butter had been set to simmer, and David's old girl friend, Mollie, had come with her mother to call.

Mollie was introduced to Gabrielle as if they had never seen each other before. Her mother, Mrs. Thompson, was so extremely polite to Gabrielle that her exaggerated good manners smacked of rudeness.

Gabrielle studied Mollie secretly as Mrs. Wesley served refreshments. No wonder David's mother looked at the girl as if she was made of sugar; she looked as if she really was. All of Mollie's coloring was as pale and fluffy as the spun candy Gabrielle bought in paper cones at the circus. If a person could judge by freckles, Mollie Thompson's face had never seen the light of sun.

Her golden curls, shaped exactly like the Cajun sausages one bought down in the bayous and ate with red beans and rice, grew from a scalp so white that it looked bloodless. Her dimity dress was exactly the same shade of pink as her round cheeks.

Gabrielle sighed to herself. She could go on forever saying nasty things to herself about this girl without dulling the sharp pangs of her envy. This was the girl David had been engaged to until he met Gabrielle and "knew he had made a mistake." But Mollie looked like anything but a mistake with her ankles neatly crossed and her hands folded in her lap. She was perfectly delicious to look at, despite the fact that her clear blue eyes showed no flash of intelligence. Like Gabrielle herself, she sat quietly with a half smile on her face as the women talked.

"The Thompsons, like the Harpers, were pioneers here in this county," Mrs. Wesley told Gabrielle. "What year did your husband's family first settle in here?"

Mrs. Thompson shrugged in a satisfied manner. "A few years before Missouri became a state in the early eighteen hundreds."

Three could play at that game as well as two, Gabrielle thought crossly. She knew her history, too. Her own mother's French family had settled in Louisiana in the 1600s. In fact, this part of the country had *all* been French until the Louisiana Purchase, which had been way back in 1803, eighteen years before Missouri was admitted into the union as a state. She held back her words more from pride than virtue.

At least the tea was delicious — minted tea — and wonderfully refreshing, with rich oatmeal cookies studded with black walnuts.

By sitting very carefully on the edge of her chair, Gabrielle kept down the itching at the backs of her legs. She could do nothing about the pain under her belt except try to keep from wriggling.

Grandma Harper had brought down a basket of quilt pieces she was sewing together into squares. Gabrielle shut her mind to Mrs. Wesley's snobbish talk and watched Grandma Harper's swift fingers join the colored patches into separate stars. Then Mrs. Wesley spoiled it all by suggesting that "the girls," Mollie and Gabrielle, walk out to see how the apple butter was coming along.

David had laid the fire inside a ring of flat stones in a barren space between the back door and the smokehouse. A three-legged black pot filled with the fragrant, spicy mass of ground apples and spices bubbled gently above the glowing coals. Daisy, her freckles practically melting and running from the heat, stood well back from the fire, stirring the rich brown mixture with a long-handled wooden paddle that looked almost like an oar from a boat.

"Are you enjoying your little visit with the Wesleys and Mrs. Harper?" Mollie asked, standing carefully out of the path of the wavering smoke.

Gabrielle nodded. "It is very pleasant here."

"And it must be very different from the style of life you are used to."

Mollie's pale eyes peered at her from under the ruffled rim of her pink bonnet. What did this fluffy creature know about life on the river? More to the point, what style of life did she think river people had?

"Very different," Gabrielle agreed. Now that they had looked at the apple butter, surely they could go back with the others.

"But you must spend *some* time on land," Mollie pressed on. "David met you on land. In the woods, I believe?"

Either the heat from the fire or Mollie's intent questioning was making the chigger bites itch again. The way Mollie had said "in the woods" made her meeting with David sound secretive and somehow evil. Gabrielle tried to keep her tone casual.

"Yes. Our boat was kept tied to shore for several days until the current went down."

Mollie laughed. "My goodness. We never think of the current except when the river reaches flood stage. I can see how David could find your strange life-style interesting. Don't you think David has an inquiring mind?"

Gabrielle fought back her rising anger. Did this creature think David was only attracted to her because she was "strange"?

"David and I liked each other at once," Gabrielle said.

Then Mollie really smiled. Two faint dimples appeared in her cheeks and her eyes became wonderfully bright. "But of course. David has always been irresistible to girls, just as his father was before him. And he does like getting to know different people. My parents think his easy way of making everyone feel important to him will make him successful in politics someday. Don't you agree?"

"I know nothing about his political aspirations," Gabrielle said, wishing her voice didn't sound so stilted and stiff.

"Oh, he has none," Mollie assured her. "But David goes through phases where he seizes on new people and new things with great enthusiasm."

This was too much.

"Are you suggesting that David's interest in me is only a passing phase?" Gabrielle asked.

Mollie raised her pale eyebrows and dropped them again, just as Mrs. Wesley often did. "Don't you?" she asked sweetly.

Then, before Gabrielle could reply, she took her skirt daintily in both hands and stepped past the smoke to start back to the house. "We probably should go back. This is our regular calling day and Mother and I still have several stops to make."

With the Thompsons gone, Gabrielle was torn between two equally strong desires. She yearned to snatch off all her clothes and dust herself all over again with the soda which had helped the stinging for a while. Yet the pain of her hunger for the river, even the sight of it, was stronger than the burning of those miserable bites.

After carrying the tray of glasses back to the kitchen for Mrs. Wesley, Gabrielle walked down the lane toward the spot from which she could see the river.

She leaned against a tree to study the river's moving face. Late-afternoon light glinted on stirring dark water, breaking into tiny points of light where the wind ruffled a pie-shaped area of water. A row of barges loaded with tree-length white lumber nudged into view, followed by a tiny tug feeding white smoke into the clear warm air. She caught her breath, straining to see the letters on the side of the tug. If she was only close enough to read the tug's name, chances were she would know the men on board. If she were on the shore, she could wave to them as all the land people did to the crafts that moved along the river.

But she was too far away. She was far from the spicy scent of the river itself, from its comforting rhythm, from her own world. And why? Because of David.

She sighed. There was the David she knew — warm, romantic, maybe a little too passionate, but loving her with a force she couldn't doubt. There was this other David who, according to Mollie, "has always been irresistible to girls, just as his father was before him," who had an "easy way of making everyone feel important to him."

What Mollie had said wouldn't have hurt so much if David himself hadn't said those puzzling things about "other girls" liking this or that.

She shivered in spite of the heat. At the crackling of twigs behind her she turned to see David, fresh from cleaning up after his work. He smiled at her in that winning way and took her in his arms.

"I should be cross at you," he said softly. "I had to look all over to find you. I should have known you were here, staring at that silly river. What can I do to make you forget it, and that boy with the crazy French name?"

She stiffened herself against him. "Nothing will ever make me forget about the river. It's my home."

"It has been your home up to now," he corrected. She would have argued, but his mouth was soft on hers and she couldn't make herself pull away.

Chapter Twelve

THE second night of Gabrielle's stay at the Wesleys', David had mentioned driving into town before supper. He had mentioned it more than once without anything coming of it. They had not gone that time, nor any day or night since. She was mostly disappointed because she had hoped to be able to buy some trinket or memento for her father and for Flossie. But she also was curious to see David's hometown, which he claimed was really great, "a classy little town."

"Is it anything like Quincy?" she asked. "Or Hannibal, or St. Louis, or Memphis?"

David flushed and mumbled something about all towns being pretty much alike. She looked at him, startled by such a ridiculous statement. Why, the river towns were as different from each other as people were.

Was it possible that he had never been in

any of the other towns along the river? Or in any other town at all, as a matter of fact, except the little village where they had met in that awful confrontation in the ice-cream parlor? To Gabrielle, this was unbelievable. The boat always made several stops going south between Hannibal, Missouri, and this place. Hannibal itself was only a hundred miles north of St. Louis by land (although much farther when you followed the winding course of the river.)

She thought of the towns along this stretch of the river. The towering cliffs and up-and-down streets of Quincy, Illinois; the endless winding caves at Hannibal, where it was said that a young girl was embalmed in copper. St. Louis was bustling and very citylike, although not anything near as charming as New Orleans or even Baton Rouge. The busy wharves at Memphis were always piled high with bulging bales of cotton by the time the *Levee Princess* got there, with banjo music thrumming in the hot muggy air. Then there was Natchez, Mississippi, with its caves along the river that used to harbor the "Under the Hill Gang" of murderers and thieves.

She only glanced away and dropped the subject, hoping that David would manage to take her to his town before her visit was over.

Gabrielle discovered why David had not taken her to town by means of a very embarrassing accident. Unfortunately, she learned at the same time how deep a wedge she had driven between David and his mother.

The two things Gabrielle loved best about the farm were the flowers and the birds. Although Mrs. Wesley grew more vegetables than flowers, the flowers she had were beautiful. An old washtub buried in the front yard spilled tiny moss roses out onto the grass. Out in back, between the chicken coop and the garden, a row of giant hollyhocks burst into fresh bloom every day. The individual blossoms looked like tiny girls dressed in full skirts, ready to dance.

No matter how amused he was by her ignorance, David was good about answering her questions. She had known the names of very few birds when she came — crows, of course, and the hawks with fringed wings that drifted above the woods beside the river. He had shown her the wrens that trilled in the house trees, and identified the bird that sang so beautifully from the fence post in the pasture as a meadowlark. When she tried to describe the tiny bird that dived in and out of the blossoms of the hollyhocks, he frowned in thought.

"Tiny," she repeated. "Smaller than a wren. They move so fast they don't seem to have wings. They hover. Oh, and they have red throats."

"Hummingbirds!" he said. "But I know why I didn't think of them right off. They're so little and so swift that people don't often see them."

"I think the hummingbirds are my favorites. They like to feed in your mother's red and pink hollyhocks," she told him.

"Not in the white flowers?" he asked, laughing at her again.

"They like the red and pink ones the best," she told him stubbornly. If he had come to travel with them on the *Levee Princess*, would she have made fun of him about things he didn't know? She doubted it, but she hated to think how Stephen DuBois and some of the other men might have reacted to his ignorance about river life.

She was sure she was right about the hummingbirds preferring the red and pink flowers. She had learned that if she stood very still in the deep shadows of the giant plants between the yard and the chicken coop, she would be completely concealed. The tiny birds either didn't see her or paid no attention to her.

Unlike the red-winged blackbirds who flew together in great noisy flocks and blackened the pasture when they came down to feed, the hummingbirds came only one or two at a time. They flew to within a few feet of a flower, hung in air a moment, then dived into the heart of a great scarlet or pink blossom.

She was there in that shadowy hiding place when David and his mother stopped and got into an argument about her.

David had apparently been on his way to the house when his mother caught him. From her first words, Gabrielle could tell she was furious. "How dare you go behind my back and get permission from your grandmother to take that girl to the barn dance tomorrow night?" she asked.

"I wanted Gabrielle to have one really good time before her father sends a buggy for her on Sunday," David said, his tone sullen. "Because of you she's been stuck here on this place during her whole visit. After the way you've acted about my taking her around anywhere, I knew for sure if I'd asked you, you'd turn me down."

"You were right. And I was right to forbid it." Her tone turned coaxing. "David, we have to live in this town. We don't need to pour grist into the gossip mill for a passing fancy like that girl. She was here, and she will be gone. If we are lucky, everyone will forget about it. Now, I want you to go right into that house and tell your grandmother you've changed your mind."

"I won't do it."

Mrs. Wesley's voice rose dangerously. "See what an evil influence that girl has had on you? First you sneak around behind my back and twist your grandmother into agreeing with your foolish notions. Then you have the gall to refuse to obey your own mother right to her face. I'm not blind, David Wesley. I see what goes on between you two. I see how you can't keep your eyes or your hands off her. She's a temptress, and she's worked her wiles on you."

David's tone was suddenly sad and a little

puzzled. "Why do you insist in acting this way about Gabrielle? She's only a lovely young girl with a different background. And I love her, Mother. I love her and intend to marry her. I told you that before you ever met her. Mollie was a good sport about it and understood. Why can't you listen to what I really want, and want it for me, too?"

"Mollie!" Mrs. Wesley said angrily. "Of course Mollie understands you, and she's willing to wait for this fever to pass. It's not as if it were the first time Mollie has had to be patient with you. Surely you remember that she was the same when you were so struck with those others — that Rosie Evans, and Abigail Farmer."

"That was different," David protested.

"The only difference is that you are now over them. And at least they were well-brought-up local girls, not some showboat actress showing her petticoats to every man on the river for the price of an admission ticket."

David broke into her words, his voice trembling in fury. "Don't *ever* talk about Gabrielle that way again."

"Now you're warning me!"

"Yes, I am warning you," he told her. "I hate to repeat myself, but I love Gabrielle and I intend to marry her. I have asked her to go to the dance with me, and Grandmother has agreed it's a good thing. Grandma doesn't like it any better than I do that we've kept her cooped up here on the farm as if we were ashamed of her."

"I *am* ashamed of her," his mother said bluntly. "She may look like other girls, but you hear the things she talks about — people using makeup and running away from home. And an actress! It's like an insult to flaunt an actress in the company of decent people."

David's voice rose ominously before he got it under control. "Now listen, Mother," he said fiercely. "I don't like that talk, and I don't like your acting as if you're doing me a favor by having Gabrielle here. Granny was the one who suggested asking her to visit, if you remember."

For some reason that Gabrielle didn't really understand, his words made his mother even angrier. "Now see here," she hissed at him, "don't go saying anything you'll regret when you've come to your senses. It's bad enough that Mrs. Forrester and the Thompsons had to come calling with her here. I'm reasonably sure we got Mrs. Forrester away without learning the truth, and Mollie and her mother are not likely to spread gossip that could affect them later."

"But they came," David reminded her triumphantly. "They wanted to see Gabrielle. My other friends do, too."

"Curiosity is a human weakness," she told him. "They'd act the same way if somebody caught Jesse James and hauled him into town. People always troop to see a spectacle.

But you are *not* taking her out among our friends, and that's the end of that."

David must have just walked away and left her because Gabrielle heard Mrs. Wesley call him to come back. After a few minutes, the back door slammed.

Gabrielle crept out from behind the wall of hollyhocks with her face flaming. David's grandmother had been right that first day in the garden. Eavesdroppers didn't hear good of themselves. But they got more questions answered than they would have thought to ask.

Maybe knowing was even worth the pain.

That night David brought the buggy around as soon as dinner was over. He held out his hand for Gabrielle to get up into the seat. As he mounted the seat beside her, he called back to the two women on the porch, "We'll be back at sundown like I promised."

"Have a nice ride," Grandma Harper called.

His mother glared after them in silence.

"Where are we going?" Gabrielle asked as the horse cantered down the lane and then turned west away from the river.

"To a very special place," he told her.

That wouldn't be the town then, Gabrielle decided. But that was all right. Who was she to pour grist into the mills of gossip?

"How do you like the house where we are living now?" David asked after a few moments of silent riding.

"I love it," Gabrielle said truthfully. "I especially like the wide porches around it and the stained-glass window above the door into the front hall."

He nodded and flipped his reins across the back of the horse, causing the animal to pick up speed. The sun was poised on the top of a ridge of trees when David turned from the main road to drive up a curving lane. When he brought the buggy to a stop, she leaned forward to look. She saw nothing but a sloping pasture studded here and there with clumps of locust trees.

"There," David said, winding the reins of the horse and turning to take her into his arms. "That is where I will build our house. Right on the crest of the hill where we will get a cross-breeze and you will have a good view of the countryside."

Gabrielle pulled away. "Please, David, don't make me angry."

He loosened his grip, but kept one arm around her shoulder. "You don't understand, do you, Gabrielle? This is my land, good, rich growing land. And it's mine to do with as I please. Grandpa Harper left it to me in his will, free and clear. You can have any house you want built here. And flowers, any kind of flowers you want to grow."

When Gabrielle remained silent, not knowing how to tell him what she had to say, he rushed on.

"But if you don't like this place, we can

always take that other house, the one we're living in now."

She stared at him in astonishment. "Your mother's house? What are you saying?"

He took her hand and kneaded it between his own. "That's Granny's house, not Mother's. Granny only lets us live there because we had no place else to go after my father took off. Granny will leave that place to me in her will. She's so crazy about you that she wouldn't mind moving if you wanted to live there right now."

"David," she said, after drawing a deep breath, "you're going too fast. I haven't said I would marry you. You mustn't make plans like that, even in your mind."

He laughed softly and seized her again, shutting off her words with a demanding kiss. She pulled back and turned away angrily. "I never said I'd marry you, and I won't even talk about it if you can't quit that."

"It's the dark guy on the boat who's making you act like this," he said.

"And stop that, too," she told him. "If you want to know one of the big things that's holding me back, it's the river. I could never live where I couldn't even see the river. Maybe I couldn't ever even live without the river under me. But I don't know yet. I really don't know."

"That's one of the big things," he said. "What else?"

She sighed. How could she tell him that she

knew how his mother felt without revealing how much she had heard?

When she had been silent a long time, he glanced at the sky and sighed, too. The sun was gone, leaving only a ruddy glow above the tops of the trees. Tiny, dark shapes dipped and darted against that band of light. Gabrielle knew they were either chimney swifts or the bats from the hill caves David had told her about earlier. She assured herself they were chimney swifts.

"I promised Granny I would be back," he said resignedly.

They rode a long time in silence. Always before he had quickly recovered his good humor after she had pushed him away. This time he was different. His tone was still angry when he finally spoke. "What else do you want from me, Gabrielle? You know you have me. You know I can never settle for another woman after you. What are you after that I haven't offered you?"

She almost gasped. Did he really think she was bargaining with him? She took a deep, steadying breath.

"I'm asking for nothing, David. I am only telling you that I am not sure I could ever live apart from the river."

The last warm sunset rays set that wonderful coppery glow on his fine face and lit his hair. How handsome he was, and how tortured he must be by what he must see as only her stubbornness. She put her hand gently on his arm.

They were at the foot of the lane. He slapped the reins hard across the horse's back. "The river," he said scathingly. "All you can think about is that stupid muddy river. A river is nothing but a watery thread that winds between the good land on its banks. The river is nothing. This is the real world."

"Your world," she told him quietly. Then they were at the front of the house.

The shadowy figure of Mrs. Wesley watched from the porch. David helped Gabrielle down in silence and left her to make her way into the house alone as he put away the horse and buggy.

Chapter Thirteen

GABRIELLE looked over her clothes a half dozen times before going to Grandma Harper's room to ask for her help.

"You couldn't put on anything you wouldn't be pretty in," Grandma Harper told her, smiling.

"But I haven't the faintest idea what anybody wears to a barn dance," Gabrielle wailed. "I've never even watched one, much less been to one."

Grandma Harper rose and put her work back into the quilting basket beside her rocking chair. "Then let's go along to your room and have a look at your things. My gracious, this is like the old times when my friends and I tried on everything but the kitchen curtains before we could decide what to sashay out in."

Grandma Harper settled in the ladder-backed chair in the guest room and watched Gabrielle lay out her dresses one by one. From outside came the clear, sweet trill of a meadowlark calling from the pasture fence.

"That deep green is mighty pretty and rich-looking," she said thoughtfully. "But as a girl I always leaned to wearing light colors to dances like this. The lights aren't that good in a barn, you know. There's no point in being there if you aren't going to be looked at."

When Gabrielle giggled in spite of herself, Grandma Harper chuckled, too. "I didn't marry me the best-looking, nicest man in this county by hanging back and getting lost in the shadows. Pull that white one out again so I can look at it better."

Gabrielle held up the dress for her inspection. The dress was one of her own favorites. The sleeves fit her slender arms to the elbow before falling in deep, loose, lace-trimmed flounces to the wrist. The bodice was trim and tailored close to her body, too, with a neckline cut straight across to barely catch on the points of her shoulders. The skirt fell in three deep tiers, each one fuller than the last and all trimmed in fine pointed lace that matched the sleeves.

"Someone stitched a lot of love into these goods," Grandma Harper said thoughtfully as she lifted the flounces and studied the small careful stitches.

"Flossie," Gabrielle told her. "She taught me to sew when I was about ten, but she only lets me make petticoats and aprons. I've never made a dress for myself. She says she dearly loves making them, and I dearly love how she does it."

"This is the one you need to wear," Grandma Harper nodded. "Now, what can we do to add a touch of color?"

"I have sashes," Gabrielle told her, "mostly with ribbons to match." She laid them out on the bedspread: pale blue, a bright clear red, and the gold that went with the green dress.

"You don't happen to have any colored petticoats, do you?" the old woman asked thoughtfully. "It's mighty attractive to see a quick peek of color when your partner swings you around."

Gabrielle had been astonished to find that Flossie had packed her bright red petticoat in with the other things. Flossie had made it for a Fourth of July show in which Gabrielle had worn all red, white, and flag blue. Gabrielle hesitated as she laid it out. "If you don't think it would be too shocking, I have this."

Grandma Harper wriggled her shoulders with delight. "Oh, my, to have such a petticoat. Does it match with that nice red sash?"

"Perfectly," Gabrielle said, holding the sash next to it. "But are you sure it would be proper to wear it?"

Grandma stiffened in her chair. "Of course I'm sure. Just because you wear a petticoat doesn't mean you're inviting anybody to look at it. But I do think red ribbons in your hair would be a touch too much. The white ones will show off those black curls better, anyway."

Gabrielle pushed the petticoat aside and slumped on the bed across from the older woman, fighting against her long training in good manners. Before she found the words for what she needed to say, Grandma Harper leaned over and put her hand on Gabrielle's knee.

"I know what's in your mind, child, and I appreciate your hesitation. You're thinking that Bertha hates you already, and wearing such a stylish outfit would only give her cause to hate you more. Forget it! You couldn't please Bertha if you went with a potato sack over your head. Nothing you do or say is ever going to change how she feels. It isn't you she hates, it's the fear of losing David to someone she can't control, of being put to shame again in her neighbors' eyes. A woman whose man walks away carries a scar that never heals. There's nothing shameful about a red petticoat. I would give a pretty penny to be able to wear one myself. Wear it for me and for David, and forget what can't be mended with that daughter of mine."

Gabrielle dropped to her knees beside the chair and hugged the old woman hard, just the way she hugged Flossie when her heart was too full of love for words. Grandma Harper patted her softly on the back with her thin, strong hands.

* * *

Gabrielle was ready too early. She had time to think of getting out the dark green dress and putting it on. But that wouldn't be fair to Grandma Harper. As she stood at the window, watching the pale moon swim up over the tops of the trees, her hands were moist with dread. She was at the point of changing the red petticoat at least two or three times before she heard the voices of the rest of the family gathering in the hall below.

She was astonished and delighted to find Grandma Harper dressed and waiting with the others. She was wearing a fine dark blue silk suit with a hint of bustle and an explosion of white lace at her throat. The white pleats inside her bonnet brim completely concealed her snow white hair. "How beautiful!" Gabrielle said.

"It was my husband's favorite," Grandma Harper said, smiling.

Mrs. Wesley would have looked wonderful, too, in her deep gray gown, if her face had not been knotted with worry.

Since the buggy seated only two in back, David helped Gabrielle up beside him in the front seat. He looked splendid in a starched white shirt under the dark, fitted jacket he had worn the night he and his mother came to the *Levee Princess*. If his mother hadn't been sitting stiffly behind Gabrielle, she would have told him how perfectly wonderful he looked.

To Gabrielle's delight, the road to the dance

led straight through town. She looked around with interest and tried to see what David found so special about it. But the town was like a dozen little settlements along the river. Shops and stores, some with false fronts rearing up against the night sky, lined the narrow dirt streets. Two churches with single white spires faced each other across the street, looking for all the world like two men braced for a fight. The inevitable sawing of locusts sounded from the trees and swirling clouds of fluttering moths circled the gas lanterns posted along the street. The only other light poured from a red-fronted saloon through whose doors also spilled the sounds of raucous laughter and pounding piano music.

Once they passed through the town, the road turned dark again, with only the buggy light to show the way. Finally they reached a lane where a boy with a lantern directed David to drive in between two lines of trees.

The barn was immense, taller than any house Gabrielle had seen outside of New Orleans. It rose straight for a great height before being crowned by a double-angled roof. Light poured from every window and door, and from clear down the lane she heard the scrape of fiddles being tuned. A long line of buggies was moving slowly past the entrance as men helped their ladies down at the broad front door. David worked the buggy through the line, assisted his grandmother and mother, then squeezed Gabrielle's hand tight as he helped her down. During that moment when their eyes met, Gabrielle felt the hammering of her heart ease off a little.

David loved her. Grandma Harper loved her. Together the two of them would keep her safe.

When David drove off to park the buggy in among the long line filling the pasture, Gabrielle stood with his mother and grandmother. A wind gauge in the form of a metal rooster creaked and swayed in the night wind. An army of barn swallows dove and swooped above the top of the barn, drawing invisible lines against a sprinkle of stars.

"There'll be little sleep for those barn swifts tonight," Grandma Harper said, following Gabrielle's eyes.

"Or for any of us," her daughter said sourly.

Grandma Harper had said there was little light at a barn dance, but coming in from the darkness, Gabrielle felt blinded for a moment. The entire center of the immense structure had been cleared to make way for dancing. At the far end, three fiddlers wearing dark suits with bright red ascots sawed and adjusted their instruments. As loud as they were, the sound was almost drowned out by the din of talk and laughter. The rest of the barn was crowded with women in great, full skirts, many wearing bonnets, and men in bright shirts and boots. Gabrielle felt her heart plunge as all the eyes in the room turned toward them in the door. David's strong arm was reassuring under her hand.

The swirl of introductions that followed dizzied Gabrielle's head. Just when she thought she had nodded and spoken to everyone in the room, a fresh couple would appear and she would hear Mrs. Wesley say again, "Our guest from out of town, Miss Prentice."

Mollie Thompson was there with a slim young man as blond as herself, whom she introduced as Glen something-or-other. Mollie must have wanted to be seen in the darkness, too. She looked like a candle flame in a clear bright yellow dress trimmed with blue ribbons the color of her eyes. Mrs. Forrester presented Gabrielle gracefully to her husband, a genial-looking man with a very red face and black handlebar moustaches.

At a table set along the wall to the left, an immense smiling woman in a dark apron stood behind a vase of red asters. The flowers were flanked by two tall crocks. She was kept busy ladling punch or lemonade from around the clear blocks of ice hiding inside the crocks. David settled his mother and grandmother on benches with a good view of the dance floor, and went to bring each of them a cool drink. Before he even got back, they were surrounded by their special friends. When David handed Gabrielle her punch, he squeezed her hand playfully. "I bet your ears are burning."

She smiled brightly, wishing she could think that was as funny as he did.

She had met only a few of this circle of

friends before the band began playing the opening grand march. She circled the floor on David's arm, regretting the red petticoat with every step. Then the caller, a large man already sweating great rings on his blue shirt, called for the first reel.

Gabrielle insisted that David let her stand with him to watch the first dance. "I don't know the steps," she told him. "I don't want to embarrass you."

"That could never happen," he told her, looking down in that tender, possessive way.

Gabrielle realized at once that, although the routine was complicated, the steps themselves were very easy. When David led her out for the second dance she quite forgot her terror in the joy of moving lightly and swiftly to the rhythm of the lively fiddling. As she was passed from hand to hand, she smiled steadily the way she always did when on stage. There was no time for conversation with any of the men who caught her, spun her for a few steps, then passed her on. She could only nod to each swift, "Good ev'ning, ma'am," or, "How de do."

The pace made her a little giddy. When David swung back to her and said this was the last dance in a "set," she was more than ready for a glass of icy punch.

While she waited beside Grandma Harper for David to make his way through the line, she idly watched the milling crowd. She saw Mollie in deep conversation with a big man who had remarkably curly hair. Before she could glance away, she saw the man turn to stare at her, narrow his eyes, and then laugh. A cold terror clutched Gabrielle again. Only Mollie and her mother, in all this roomful of strangers, knew who she was and where she was from. But Mrs. Wesley had been so sure that Mollie would protect the secret for her own reasons. Suddenly, Gabrielle was just as sure Mrs. Wesley was wrong.

David handed her the cup of punch and led her toward the cool air coming in at the wide open door. "That red underskirt of yours is getting a lot of attention," he told her, his tone only half amused.

"Your grandmother picked it out," she told him.

He shrugged. "I guess I should have known. Just so my mother knows that's why you decided to wear it."

It was always back and forth with David. She didn't try to hide her annoyance as she turned to face him. "Don't you like the way I look, David?"

He flushed and would have reached for her if they had not been surrounded by other couples. "You know I love the way you look, Gabrielle. I would rather look at you, touch you, than anything in life. It's just that. . . ."

Maybe it was fortunate that the music began again, drowning out his words.

By the end of the next set a huge display of cookies and cakes had been added to the refreshment table. The gingerbread, huge fragrant squares with sticky tops, went first, followed by the chocolate cakes and other kinds. Gabrielle couldn't possibly hold all of the big wedge of angel cake David brought her, but he was happy to finish eating it for her.

"You sure dance like a flying thistle for somebody who's never done it before," he told her, his tone a little doubting.

"I've danced all my life," she reminded him.

"But this is different," he told her.

"Not so much. You stay with the music and keep moving your feet. The steps aren't hard."

"Some find them so," he said, almost grumpily.

"Would you like it better if I stumbled around out there?" she asked.

He shook his head. "Now, don't fly off, Gabrielle. I just can't stand seeing those other men touching you to swing you around."

This is the last set, Gabrielle reminded herself as the music began again and David's hand was warm at the back of her waist as he led her out. This is the last set and tomorrow my father will send for me and this will all be over. Not until that moment had she realized how carefully she had counted the days, almost the hours, until this visit was over.

The set went swiftly in spite of the gleaming faces and flushed cheeks of the dancers. It was almost to an end when, between numbers, the caller rapped loudly on the post beside the band and shouted, "Announcement! Clarence Young has an announcement!"

As the crowd stilled where they stood, Gabrielle watched Mollie's friend, the large man with the very curly hair, take the caller's place. She gripped David's arm and he looked down at her, confused.

"Ladies and gentlemen," the man called out in a voice that surely would have brought the cows in from the field. "We've got a real treat here tonight, an actress and singer who performs for money instead of just the fun of it. A professional, right in our midst." He paused a moment to let the flurry of excited comment settle down.

"What say we ask her to honor us with a song?" As he spoke, he pointed with a dramatic gesture toward Gabrielle and David. "There she is herself, Mademoiselle Gabrielle of the *Levee Princess*."

A thunder of applause followed his words, and people shouted, "Hear, hear" and, "Let's have a song!"

Gabrielle felt herself flush the color of her own petticoat. What should she do? What *could* she do? She dared not even glance toward Mrs. Wesley. David's hand clamped like an iron vise on her arm.

"Don't do it," he said fiercely. "Just smile and shake your head as if there's some mistake."

"But there's not," she said. "That man even has my name."

"If you have no shame for yourself, think of me," he pleaded. "Think of our life together and how hard it will be to live this down once they know what you are."

His words were like a cold bath. She turned to stare at him in disbelief as the crowd kept clapping and calling.

"What am I, David?" she asked quietly.

As David's face paled, the man with the curly hair was there, holding his arm out, smiling at her with a kind of curious triumph. Mollie had told him. She had seen Mollie tell him. She glanced around. It should be easy enough to locate that bright yellow figure in the crowd. Gabrielle turned and stared at Mollie directly for a long moment before taking the man's arm and accompanying him to the platform where the fiddlers waited.

The men quit stamping and the women fell silent as she stood before them. Suddenly a new voice spoke at her side. The caller, his shirt drenched now but his face wreathed with smiles, pushed the curly-haired man aside to stand beside Gabrielle.

"Listen, folks," he said without concealing his excitement, "what we have here is not just another showboat actress. This little lady is Captain Joshua Prentice's daughter. There's not a singer on the five rivers better loved or more respected than this little lady.

Most of you can remember when this river was flooded with tramp boats, with gamblers and medicine men, and girly shows passing themselves off for entertainment. You remember our standing at the wharf with guns and clubs, driving those varmints on down-river? Then Captain Prentice came along with his *Levee Princess*. You know what kind of a boat the captain runs — family entertainment you could take the preacher to and not give him grist for a sermon. We have here the queen of the river, for all that she's little more than a child. What a treat for all of us!"

As he spoke, he took Gabrielle's hand and shook it vigorously. "Honored, my dear, I'm honored. Now what will you sing for the folks?"

Gabrielle loved that loud fat man, sweat and all, with her whole heart for that moment. As she had walked forward on the arm of the curly-haired man who had been Mollie's accomplice, she had thought for one furious moment that she would stand up there and sing one of the bawdy songs she had heard in Memphis or New Orleans, the kind of songs her father never allowed in any of his shows. But as the caller released her hand and stepped back with a deep bow from the waist, she knew what song she would sing.

She stood a moment, helpless, not knowing what to do with her hands. "Wait!" the caller cried. "Wait right there, mademoiselle."

She saw him work his way through the crowd, lift the bunch of red asters from the pitcher on the refreshment table, shake the water from their stems, and start back. She smiled with delight. This was a man who knew show business, who knew what props an ingenue singer always held during her songs.

She took the flowers in her arms, curtsied her thanks, and spoke to the crowd in the clear voice that her father had trained so carefully.

"Ladies and gentlemen," she said, bowing slightly. "Members of the band." She nodded to them. "Tomorrow I return to my home on the *Levee Princess* after enjoying the hospitality of your community. I will be proud to tell my father about all of you and the honor you've paid him and his showboat. Because of the pride we *all* feel in what we do, I want to sing for you the last song my mother, who was also a singer and composer, wrote before her death. She called it 'Mighty Mississippi, River of Dreams.'"

When Gabrielle sang this song on the boat she was softly accompanied by Flossie on the dulcimer. Now she must bring the magic of her mother's love for the river alive with no help at all.

Clinging to the still-dripping bouquet of flowers, she began the tender ballad, softly at first, then with her voice swelling to fill the rafters of that great room. She had never sung better and she knew it. She had never sung with tears closer to falling, either. As the song drew to a close, in the soft, final, loving farewell, the crowd stood silent.

As she said, "Thank you," and looked out over that sea of faces, she saw glistening cheeks that matched her own.

The caller himself ushered her back to David's side with wild applause still vibrating all over the room. Mollie turned aside her pink face, red now with anger, but as Gabrielle passed Grandma Harper's chair, the old woman caught at her dress. Gabrielle leaned to kiss her cheek. When she passed on, her lips were salty with the old woman's tears.

The evening was over almost at once. Gabrielle nodded and shook hands steadily as David steered her toward the merciful darkness and privacy of the humming night.

It was almost as if Mrs. Wesley had given up on her war against Gabrielle. They all rode in silence during the long drive home, through the sleeping town, and up the lane to the house. Only Grandma Harper could be heard humming softly to herself once in a while from the backseat of the buggy.

"Wait for me," David whispered as he let her off at the door. Mrs. Wesley stomped upstairs without a word, but Grandma Harper kissed Gabrielle good night before leaving her waiting on the porch for David.

For the first time Gabrielle sat in Grandma Harper's chair and began to rock gently. The softest kind of breeze fanned her face as she looked for the moon, now poised on the far horizon. A night bird, whose name she didn't know, trilled from the trees along the lane, and the yard and pasture bloomed with fireflies.

It was almost over, leaving her with memories she would always cherish.

And lessons she must never forget.

David took her hands and pulled her to her feet. "How wonderful you were tonight," he said. "I should have known that magic of yours would work even here. But, really, Gabrielle, once we're married — "

"David," she interrupted firmly. "There will be no marriage, not between us. It wouldn't work."

"But you love me," he said, urgently seeking her lips. "I know you love me."

"I do love you," she admitted, turning her head aside. "But not enough. And you love me in the wrong way."

"What do you know about how I feel?" he asked angrily. "How can anyone love the wrong way?"

She sighed. If she tried to explain, he would only argue and never really understand, anyway. Maybe a showboat person couldn't ever explain to a land person. But he was no different from anyone else in the audience on the showboat. She had attracted him by the magic of the tightrope act. He would not accept her as a real person. He would want her to be like his mother and Mollie on the surface, and only be herself secretly and privately, as if in shame. The true Gabrielle would be buried somewhere, hidden and miserable and bitter at being rejected.

"But you came here," he protested with growing annoyance. "It was like a promise for you to come."

"A visit," she reminded him. "This was always only a visit for us to get to know each other better."

"So you didn't like me after you knew me," he said sullenly.

There was no reason to hurt him. "Do you like me as much as you did when I came?" she asked.

He was silent for a moment, then put his head against hers and held her close. "But I want you," he insisted.

When she slid from his arms to go inside, she heard his muffled, angry mutter, and smiled to herself. It was better that she leave him angry with her than sick with sorrow.

Chapter Fourteen

ALTHOUGH Gabrielle had no idea what time the buggy would arrive to take her home, she woke well before the first crow of the bronze-colored rooster. She forced herself to lie still in bed for a long time. She was already dying of impatience. Being up and dressed could only make her more restless to leave.

Yet, as eager as she was to go home, she felt a strange sadness. Even if David were an easier person to deal with, even if his mother had welcomed her as warmly as Grandma Harper had, she had still lost her childhood dream. She wasn't a land person and never could be.

Thinking about that childhood dream brought a line of poetry into her mind. She struggled to remember where it came from. She had never realized until this trip how many words from plays and songs and poems she had memorized without even meaning to.

Suddenly it came back to her. She could see Flossie on stage reciting the poem with her hands clasped tightly before her. The poem was called "Love and Duty" and was very popular at the patches along the Tennessee River.

One line of the poem asked a question: "Was my dream, then, a shadowy lie?"

Gabrielle sat up and pulled the sheet around her shoulders. Her own dream had been exactly that! Flossie had told her about falling in love with the showboat first, and then with Lance because he was part of it. Could Gabrielle have done the same thing with David? Had all those years of dreaming about living on land prepared her to respond to David in that wildly emotional way when she didn't love him at all, except for the fact that he was a land person who swept her away with his reckless courting?

She clutched the sheets tightly. How lucky she had been to discover her mistakes before she made any promises she would be forced to keep. She knew what her father thought of people who failed to keep their pledges. Then she remembered that, according to David's own testimony, he had made promises to Mollie that he later broke.

She thought of David's family sleeping in the quiet house.

Poor Mrs. Wesley dreamed that by saying David was like his famous grandfather, she could keep him from being a weak man like his own father had been.

And David himself dreamed of having both a butterfly of his own and what he called "a proper life" at the same time.

Grandma Harper was different. She alone was not fooled by dreams that were shadowy lies. Instead of dreaming, she had only hoped that Gabrielle would stay and be a changing force for David. But more than that, she had been wise and generous in accepting Gabrielle's decision.

Thinking about Grandma Harper hurt the most. How awful it was to think she might never see that wonderful old woman again. Just thinking about it made her so restless that she shoved back the sheets and got up. If only her father could know Grandma Harper. They would love each other, she knew they would.

After she finished dressing, Gabrielle set her packed trunk inside the door of her room. Carrying her shoes, she tiptoed carefully down the stairs in her stockinged feet and let herself out the front door. The black dog was sleeping in a bare spot under the black walnut tree. He raised his head to blink sleepily and thump the earth with his tail before settling down again. The rooster began to crow groggily as she stared down the lane where the buggy would come.

What if something happened to the boat and her father couldn't get away to come get her? David had driven all day to get them from Mistress Barnes' house to the farm when she came. The boat would be even farther downriver now. What if a buggy couldn't get here in a day, or if they couldn't find the right lane even when they were close?

As she had every day since David had shown her the way, she walked toward the bend of the path where she could catch that small glimpse of the Mississippi River. As she stood staring at the glinting, changeable face of that distant water, she heard the sleepy stamp of a horse's hoof, very near.

She jumped, startled. Then she remembered that David never let the horses into the pasture behind this row of trees. But who could be passing along the road at this hour of the morning?

For a long moment she stared down the dusky lane, half afraid. Then, gathering up her courage, she walked only a few steps more and saw a solitary horse standing in the traces of a black buggy. The horse turned its head at her approach and nickered softly. At the sound, a woman's bonnet appeared around the hood of the buggy. Gabrielle cried out in joy and ran toward the buggy as fast as she could.

Flossie!

After several ecstatic hugs, Gabrielle drew back. "But how early you are! This is wonderful."

"Whoever sleeps after three?" Flossie asked with a laugh. "And, anyway, we stayed a night over on the way. We wanted to get an early enough start to get back to the *Levee Princess* by sundown."

The other half of the "we" was Stephen DuBois. "I came along to drive," he said with that familiar half smile. Gabrielle smiled back at him, but quickly looked away, remembering again David's ridiculous comment that Stephen was in love with her.

"It's a very good thing he did," Flossie told her, smiling at Stephen. "I must say he's managed to impress me. I've been a showboat person so long that these contraptions scare me to death."

Gabrielle giggled. "You should have heard these people when they found out I didn't even know how to ride a horse."

Flossie sniffed. "I wager nothing was said about the many things you can do that they don't even know half about!"

Gabrielle had barely caught up on the news from home before the morning sounds made it apparent that the people of the farm were up, starting their day. "Why don't you bring your horse up to the barn?" she asked Stephen. "I know Mrs. Wesley will offer you breakfast. You could unhitch him for hay and water while we are eating."

Stephen exchanged an amused glance with Flossie and laughed genially. "Listen to that! In only a week she has learned to talk like a farmer."

Gabrielle was amazed that in spite of his teasing words, his tone held none of that bit-ing sarcasm she had always resented so much.

Mrs. Wesley's cordial greeting to Flossie and Stephen telegraphed her relief that Gabrielle was leaving. David shook hands with Flossie and tipped a curt nod to Stephen, but Grandma Harper made no secret of her delight at meeting the new arrivals.

"I can't tell you how much I have enjoyed this young lady," she told Flossie. "And I have her own testimony that she owes her good education and grace to you."

Flossie gave Gabrielle a flustered glance.

"I told her about you," Gabrielle explained, "and how like a mother you had been to me."

Flossie grinned at the older woman. "Now mind you, I claim only the *good* things she has learned."

"And you, Mr. DuBois," Grandma Harper asked. "Are you a member of the show cast, too?"

Mrs. Wesley interrupted with a strained smile. "Mother, I'm sure these travelers would rather have breakfast and be on their way than spend time in social chatter."

Gabrielle enjoyed that last breakfast better than any meal she had eaten on the farm. She knew where the ham hung in the smokehouse that produced the delicious round slices of meat sizzling in the big iron skillet. She had heard the chickens brag about laying the very eggs that Mrs. Wesley broke into the red fat around the ham. Best of all, she liked eating the rosy sauce from the giant rhubarb plants that lined the garden fence.

But in spite of Mrs. Wesley's disapproval, a steady current of social chatter flowed between Flossie and Grandma Harper. Ignoring the stiff silence between the two young men, Grandma Harper forgot her food to lean forward, bright-eyed, and fire questions at Flossie about the seasons of the year on the *Levee Princess*. "Are the other rivers you travel different from the Mississippi?" the old woman asked.

Flossie laughed. "Like night and day. The Ohio River is like a rocking chair next to this one. The only river harder to navigate is the Missouri, and we don't even try that one."

"So you leave Cincinnati in the early spring and travel until late winter?"

Flossie nodded. "We go up the Kanawha River and the Monongahela. That's mining country and the people live in little patches or settlements along the river, so the wet spring mud doesn't keep them from coming to the shows. Then we play Pittsburgh. That city is famous among showboat people as being the worst town to work on all the rivers, yet we seldom give a showboat performance anywhere without using at least one song by Pittsburgh's native son, Stephen Foster."

"Then you come back up the same way?" Grandma Harper asked.

"Oh no, we come down the Ohio and just

dip into the other rivers along there — the Kentucky, the Wabash, the Tennessee, and the Green River — before reaching the Mississippi again."

Gabrielle felt Mrs. Wesley's disapproving glance on her, but she didn't care. "Then we change directions," she told Grandma Harper. "After working up and down the Illinois River, we go clear north to Minneapolis and work our way back down south like we are doing now."

"We always plan to finish the year in Louisiana in the bayous, or Baton Rouge, where there is no danger from river ice," Flossie explained.

The old woman sighed. "What a waste that I was born here and shall die without traveling more than fifty miles from this place. Even the names of your rivers are like music."

"You have no cause to regret a virtuous and proper life, Mother," her daughter rebuked her.

All this while Stephen and David had eaten in surly silence, not exchanging so much as a word. When Grandma Harper realized that everyone else was through eating, she lay her napkin by her plate. "My gracious, I'm keeping you all." She rose. "Come, Gabrielle, I want to send some fresh herbs home with you from my garden."

Gabrielle found it strange to walk that familiar path and know she was doing it for the last time. But everything seemed unchanged since she came. The hollyhocks still bloomed on their giant stalks; the dusty chickens still scratched and scolded in the coop; and hidden locusts droned in the yard trees. A shift in the wind carried the acrid stench of the barnyard their way, and a horse raised its head from the water trough to stare at them.

Once away from the house, Grandma Harper slid her hand in under Gabrielle's arm. "I grieve to see you go, my child," she said quietly. "I grieve for myself, but most of all for David. I saw you at once as the girl who could be the making of him. But at what a cost to you! He is too like his father for my taste. But even if he were to change and be faithful and loyal to you, you would always hunger for those rivers. And who's to blame you? Your place is on that water. Tell me something about that dark-eyed young man who watches you with such loving eyes."

Gabrielle, caught off guard, didn't know what to say. "He's very talented but you are mistaken about the loving eyes. He really can't stand me, and makes no secret of it."

The old woman's laugh was merry. "How can you be so wise and still so innocent? There is no better testament to his love than that he sat all through breakfast wishing my grandson would drop dead."

At Gabrielle's shocked expression, Grandma Harper patted her arm. "Time will loosen his tongue. And I am sure he will not make of you what David's father made of my daughter — a bitter, lonely woman thrown on the charity of her own family."

Her voice changed as she handed Gabrielle a pair of shears from her pocket. "Now cut a little of that first bush and tie it with this string. This is rosemary . . . which is also for remembrance." Gabrielle was startled to see Grandma Harper's eyes moist with tears.

David insisted on carrying Gabrielle's trunk to the buggy without help. She walked along beside him, thanking him again for the hospitality he and his family had shown her.

"You know that when you came I intended you to stay with me forever," he told her softly. "I must have been mad to hope that you might learn to love me as I do you." He paused and looked at her in that intent way that almost frightened her. "We could try again, you know. Granny, particularly, would welcome you with open arms. She doesn't often take to people the way she did to you."

With her head still full of Grandma Harper's amazing words, Gabrielle listened to David thoughtfully. He was still as loving as always, but with a new hesitation. Behind his words she heard more than he had meant her to hear. His hopes were in the past and had not been realized. His were the words of a disappointed suitor a little bit relieved to be free of a difficult situation.

"We will both have our memories," she told him. He nodded and looked at her. She had an eerie feeling that she knew what he was seeing as his eyes held hers. He had forgotten again that she was an ordinary girl with a mind of her own and her heart pledged to the river. In his eyes she was once more a butterfly, that floating dream of a girl high in the dappled shadow of an oak grove, a shadowy lie in a dream from which he might never awaken now. Gabrielle felt a moment's pity for Mollie Thompson. It was almost impossible to compete with a dream. Mollie would have her work cut out for her.

For the first few miles they traveled downriver, Flossie chattered like the catbird in the gooseberry bushes. She was full of gossip, tidbits of news from old friends they had met, funny things that had happened on board, and how proud Tom Luce had been to catch a fish that reached from his fingertips clear to his elbow. When Flossie fell silent, Gabrielle glanced back and realized she had dropped off to sleep.

Stephen laughed softly. "I wonder that she lasted this long. But she's a game one. She stayed awake all the way up here from nervousness about the horse. When I teased her about it, she told me that a watched horse never bolts. I guess having two farmers in the buggy made her feel more relaxed."

"Two farmers?" Gabrielle asked. Then, remembering his teasing earlier, she asked, "Don't tell me you were a farmer, too?"

"What else?" he said, smiling over at her. Why did she keep remembering what both

David and his grandmother had said about Stephen's feeling for her? She was glad he looked back at the road before the color flushed into her face.

"You've heard a half dozen stories like mine," he went on. "I was raised just out of Natchez on a plantation that bordered the Mississippi. I never saw a plume of smoke rise from a steamboat on that river that I didn't drop my plow or my cotton sack and run for the riverbank. I hated the eternal dryness of land as much as I hated the muddy rains. I despised the way the heat rose in waves from the baked earth. I even hated the smell of the cotton bolls splitting open in the fields, never mind that was where our money came from. I didn't care how I got to be a riverman. I only wanted the dust of land off my feet."

"So how did you do that?" she asked.

"The hard way," he said. "When I was a little past twelve, I talked a captain into taking me on as a deckhand for five dollars a week plus board. The most exciting thing I ever did was stand at the end of a gangplank to throw a coil of rope over a post to secure the boat. But I worked at studying the river until I got to be a cub pilot the year I was fifteen. I might have done that forever if I hadn't seen my first showboat. That hooked me good! I nearly killed myself that next year learning gymnastics and then dancing. I was sixteen — your age, I guess — when I got my first job on a showboat."

"But you sing, too," Gabrielle reminded him.

He laughed. "Monkey see, monkey do! Once it's in your blood, it's there to stay. I even know enough magic tricks to be able to help the captain during his act."

Gabrielle nodded, but his words brought a pang. She hadn't even thought to wonder who had taken her place in the magic act.

The miles went easily. They passed dusty groves of deep green and orchards like the one whose chiggers still itched when she got too warm. They passed pastures of cattle, and fields where farmers worked at harvesting. Stephen was full of good river stories, and he always told them with himself as the butt of the joke. This habit reminded her of her father, who had always been big enough to admit publicly that he was capable of making mistakes.

When her father had hired Stephen DuBois, she had been delighted. He was young like herself. At last she would have a young friend. For the first time since those disappointing weeks after he came aboard, that hope came back.

"So this is what you want to do all your life?" she asked him.

He looked at her in surprise. "Not altogether," he told her. "One day I mean to own a showboat of my very own."

"Have you ever talked about this with my father?" she asked.

He grinned over at her, nodding. "The captain has given me lots of encouragement. He just the same as told me he was working toward expanding and running two boats on the rivers. He showed me the plans and said you knew them like the back of your hand. He told me that if I learned the ropes and passed the exam for a pilot's license, maybe he'd have a boat for me himself."

"I intend to get a pilot's license, too," she told him.

He turned to study her thoughtfully. "Can a girl do that?" he asked.

She grinned. "Father and I think we might be able to pull it off. We studied the rules. They don't say a girl can, but neither do they say she can't."

He laughed warmly as Flossie spoke sleepily from the backseat. "I wouldn't want to suggest that the conversation was dry up there in front, but I would give my best ruffled petticoat for a cold drink."

"I've seen that petticoat, Stephen." Gabrielle laughed. "Let's find a village or something fast before she lowers her bid."

He smiled and looked over at her, his dark eyes wondrously gentle. "As good as done," he told her. "From the way the farmhouses have been getting closer together, I'd guess you could figure on winning a new petticoat in less than a half hour."

Chapter
Fifteen

As Gabrielle turned to look back at Flossie, the road they were following emerged from the deep shade of the woods to pass into brilliant sunshine. When Flossie had settled herself for her nap, she had untied her bonnet strings. The bonnet had fallen back on her shoulders, exposing her hair. The sun struck the soft curls that had fallen over her forehead, adding golden glints to their already marvelous fire. Her bonnet strings, the same sea green color as her dress, spilled in a delicious tumble over the wide white collar that framed her smooth throat. Gabrielle smiled tenderly at her friend. Flossie looked like a carefully posed picture there in the backseat of the buggy. The pose was perfect even to the way her graceful hands were placed on the seat to brace her body against the swaying of the buggy.

But the words Gabrielle had meant to say stuck in her throat. She could not believe her eyes. Pressed onto the seat of the buggy under Flossie's hand lay a handbill, the kind of show program Bony carefully printed out on his little press in the corner by the dining room. Gabrielle stared at the handbill in horror a moment before managing to speak. She made a special effort to keep the trembling she felt out of her voice. "May I see that, Flossie?" she asked carefully.

Flossie yawned a little as she leaned to hand the piece of slightly crumpled paper to Gabrielle.

Gabrielle could not control the shaking of her hands as she read the handbill carefully. Her eyes had not deceived her. The handbill was just like the ones Bony had printed for her great act, except for two very important details.

The figure walking the tightrope across the top of the handbill was now that of a man carrying a baton instead of a parasol.

And the line of bold letters read:

MONSIEUR ETIENNE IN HIS DEATH-DEFYING TIGHTROPE WALK.

Etienne was the French spelling for Stephen!

Gabrielle knew exactly what she had to do.

She turned to Stephen, her voice uneven with fury. "Stop this buggy." When he only frowned at her in confusion, she repeated her words, this time in a genuine shout. "Stop this buggy this minute! I want out! I won't ride another mile. . . ."

He heard her all right, he couldn't help it. But instead of obeying her command, he paid no attention. He slapped the reins briskly across the horse's back so that it picked up speed.

"Gabrielle," Flossie called from the back-seat. "What on earth is the matter? What are you shouting about?"

"As if you didn't know!" Gabrielle cried as she gathered her skirts in her hands and slid along the seat toward the buggy door. "If you two can't figure this out, you are as stupid as you are traitorous. Whichever way it is, I'm not riding another mile with either one of you."

The buggy careened rapidly along the rutted road as she summoned her courage to jump out. The nerve of that Stephen DuBois! It was bad enough that he had stolen her act, now he was trying to keep her a prisoner against her will.

Never mind how scared she was. Never mind that the masses of flowering shrubs along the wayside could easily hide rocks, or snakes, or any number of other dangerous things. She clapped one hand on her bonnet, clutched her full skirt with the other, and slid to the end of the buggy seat, braced and ready to jump.

"No," Stephen cried frantically, realizing what she was planning. "No, Gabrielle, no!"

He jerked the horse's reins too quickly. The animal panicked. As Gabrielle jumped free, she heard the horse neigh crazily as it reared in the traces. Stephen was trying to speak soothingly to it, using all his strength to get the frantic animal under control while Flossie squealed in terror from the backseat.

Gabrielle, free of the buggy, tumbled into a clump of fading asters and rolled a few feet before she could stop herself. While Stephen still fought to subdue the horse, she leaped to her feet and began to run. She was glad to hear the horse still whinnying wildly behind her. That only gave her a better head start in getting away. Her very teeth were jolted by the fall, but she was too mad to care. Maybe she had grown past crying with unhappiness, but fury still brought a wild rush of tears to her eyes.

She hadn't stopped running when she heard the buggy shudder to a rattling stop. Then Stephen came crashing through the brush behind her. He caught up with her at once and seized her by the shoulders.

"Let me go, you snake," she shouted, trying to wriggle free of his grasp. "Men! You're all alike — all alike and all sickening."

"Shut up," he said fiercely, shaking her. "Shut up just one minute and listen."

Listen. She was flooded with shame at all the listening she had done already. Oh, the humiliation of those wonderful, brief miles when she had been stupid enough to listen to his confidences, to believe they could ever be friends. And all that time she had been hanging on his words with sympathy and trust, he had been hiding the miserable fact that he had gone behind her back and stolen her act on her father's own boat!

"Thief," she told him angrily. "You're a thief and a low life and you've taken advantage of my father as well as me." As she spoke, she struggled in his arms. He was strong, but she wasn't a dancer for nothing. She bent swiftly and twisted herself free of his grasp. She plunged away, fighting to keep her balance. Almost at once she was through the woods and facing an open fenced field. She dropped to the ground, rolled under the fence, and stood up, gasping, on the other side. Then she turned to face him, horrified to realize that her eyes were streaming tears in spite of herself.

"Now," she told him, "get back to that buggy and go home, both of you."

The last thing she expected was for him to obey her. Yet for a moment, he seemed to be doing just that. He stopped at the edge of the trees where she left him and stood looking at her with the strangest, almost fearful look on his face.

"Gabrielle," he said quietly, almost in a whisper.

"Leave!" she told him angrily. "Go on. Get back to the boat and river. I can take care of myself!"

"Gabrielle," he whispered again, his tone full of warning. "Gabrielle, listen to me.

Don't look around and don't shout. Just move very slowly and come back under that fence again. But do it quickly, Gabrielle. Quickly!"

A blue jay squawked wildly in a willow nearby as she heard the other sound for the first time. She felt the vibration of heavy hoofbeats drumming on the earth at almost the same second. She turned to see an immense black bull, its head lowered, snorting as it pounded its way toward her from across the pasture.

For a moment she couldn't even move. Pure terror turned her legs into something quivering and helpless. Stephen must have sensed her panic, for he ran to the fence and vaulted it to land at her side. He grabbed her as if she were a rag doll and pushed her down on the ground and under the fence. In a minute he was outside the fence with her, pulling her to her feet, brushing the dirt and leaves from her face and hair, whispering her name over and over.

The bull stopped a few feet short of the fence with an infuriated roar. It pawed the earth, ripping grass with its sharp hooves. It backed off a few feet and lowered its head again, snorting with anger.

Stephen put both arms around Gabrielle and began to walk slowly backward away from the fence. She had the sense that Stephen was holding his breath as they moved into the shadows at the edge of the woods.

"There's no point in testing the old wood in those fence rails," he whispered. "Easy now. Keep coming! Back up!"

The bull raised its head, looked at them one way and then another before turning to walk away. A few yards off, it turned to look their way again, snorting a little. Stephen held her very close and very still. "It's hard for it to see us in this shadow unless we move," he whispered. He must have been right, because in a moment the animal pawed the ground, snorted a few times, walked away a few yards, and dropped its head to begin grazing.

"Whew," Stephen said, dropping his arms.

"I hate cows," she said, wishing her voice wouldn't squeak like that. "And bulls," she added after a minute. "And horses, and pigs, and chickens, especially roosters."

Stephen was smiling down at her in that lopsided way that she shouldn't still find attractive after the way he had treated her.

"Thank you for that," she said after a minute. "But nothing has changed. You're still a thief and a low life who took advantage of me the minute I turned my back."

Flossie was coming through the woods, calling.

"She wants you to get back in the buggy," Stephen told her calmly.

"And I want you to give me one reason why I should. It was bad enough that before I even left that boat everybody was telling me how they would get along just fine without me. But I had no idea that the minute I got off, you would grab my act and take top billing."

Flossie, her bonnet now hanging halfway down her back, stopped a few feet away from them.

"Wait right there, Gabrielle Prentice," she said firmly. "You want one reason why you should quit acting like a common scold? I'll name you that reason: Captain Joshua Prentice, he's your reason."

Gabrielle stared from Flossie to Stephen. "You're making that up."

Flossie grabbed for her bonnet and rammed it back on her head. "Tell her, Stephen," she ordered.

Stephen's expression was sober and his eyes were pleading. "Nobody planned for this to happen, Gabrielle. You have to remember that news travels along the shore like a log rides the river current. At our next stop downriver, the crowd was furious. They told the captain how many miles they had traveled to see the tightrope-walking act. They asked for their money back. Then when they thought about the trouble they had gone to to get there, they threatened to get their money back double if they had to beat it out of the crew."

Flossie nodded to assure her what Stephen said was true.

"That's when your father asked me to try to fill in for you. I am a gymnast, you know, and there's not too big a jump between what

I have always done and tightrope-walking. The boat stayed over that next night and I did my first show. It wasn't any great performance, but it satisfied the people who had been so threatening the night before."

"Did Father have to let them all in free?" she asked, knowing how her father hated to be bullied into anything.

He nodded, then grinned that half-embarrassed way. "But let's face the facts, Gabrielle. I'm nothing like as much fun to look at as you are. I had to add a little to the act to make it worth their money."

"Add a little?" Gabrielle asked. "What does that mean?"

"Part of the way he rope-walks on his hands," Flossie explained. "And that's why I brought that handbill along. Your father has this wonderful idea — "

"Could we talk about the new act in the buggy?" Stephen asked. "Captain Prentice is going to be pacing the deck with his binoculars, watching for us to get back."

Flossie reached for Gabrielle's hand. "Come on, love," she coaxed. "Give your father a chance."

Her father! It hadn't occurred to her that anyone but Stephen himself had come up with that traitorous idea. But her father was right. Stephen could do anything with his superb balance and slender, muscular body. Lost in thought, she let Stephen lead her back to the buggy. When she looked at him, he was watching her soberly.

"I'm really sorry, Stephen," she said. "I feel like an absolute fool for having lost my temper like that. Forgive all those things I said. I just didn't know."

Instead of untying the reins, Stephen put his arm across the back of her seat and leaned toward her. "Then you didn't really mean them?" he asked quietly.

She shook her head. "I was angry and I didn't know."

"A few minutes ago I was congratulating myself that we might finally become friends," he told her. "Now that doesn't satisfy me. I've already told your father that if you decided against that land person and came back to us, I wanted his permission to try to persuade you to marry me."

When she gasped in astonishment, he laughed softly. "Oh, Gabrielle," he said. He shook his head and took her gently by both shoulders. "You are so skilled at what you do, and act the lady that you are so much of the time that I forget how young you are. If you had known anything at all about men, you would have known that I couldn't stand to be near you because I was out-of-my-mind in love with you. I couldn't listen to you sing without wanting to kill every man in the room for hearing you, too."

"But, Stephen," she cried. What could she say? Maybe he didn't need to know how much his angry treatment had hurt her. But the very thought that he cared that much made her breath quicken.

"I guess I thought I had forever," he went on quietly. "I knew from the very beginning how deeply your father loved you. I knew I had to prove myself to him first. I had to wait until he knew I was serious, both about you and about being a showboat captain. I was terrified that he might turn me down, maybe even throw me off the boat." He grinned down at her. "I have your father's permission to court you. Now I need yours."

From the backseat, Flossie spoke quietly. "I can see the billing now: Madame Gabrielle and Monsieur Etienne in the Death-Defying ... and so forth."

Gabrielle looked at him. She had always thought him talented, and one of the handsomest men she'd ever seen, but she had never seen him like this, gentle and maybe a little fearful of what answer she might give.

David, smiling and confident, was suddenly full in her mind. "I almost always get my way," he had told her.

Did she want Stephen to court her? She certainly hadn't wanted David to! How many times had she told him she didn't know him well enough even to talk about marriage? But Stephen was different from David in so many ways — all of them good. She and Stephen shared so many things: their pride in the work they did, their respect for her father, and their mutual dreams of spending their lives on the river.

There wasn't any really ladylike way to give an honest answer. It wouldn't be honest to tell him no, but neither did she want to be rushed and pushed again. She raised her eyes to Stephen's and saw something special there, a patience that said he felt she was worth waiting for. He was really willing to court her, not try to sweep her off her feet with elaborate praise, warm embraces, and the offer of fine houses and land. Not until the words were out did she realize how prim she sounded. "I think I would enjoy that very much, Stephen."

Flossie laughed from the backseat. "What a disappointment. I thought I would be forced to get out and walk about a mile up that road while you started this heavy courting."

Stephen smiled back at her. "Forget the walk up the road, Flossie. Gabrielle and I understand each other. If you want to create something to last forever, you don't try to throw it together overnight."

As he spoke, he leaned to Gabrielle. It was wonderful to feel Stephen's lips touch hers gently, to feel his arm close around her protectively and feel safe and comfortable there.

And when she and Stephen knew each other well enough and decided that it was time, she wouldn't wonder if she was turning to him to escape anything the way she had with David. When that day came, she would be turning to him only for love.

Flossie sighed from the backseat. "Very well. If there's not going to be a grand finale,

I might as well take another nap. But don't forget that I'm dying of thirst back here."

Stephen laughed softly as he brought the horse to a brisker canter. Reaching over, he laid his free hand over Gabrielle's on the seat between them, and smiled at her with eyes as deep as the river.

Coming next from Sunfire: MERRIE, *who is a stowaway aboard the* Mayflower, *finds love and adventure in the New World.*

SUNFIRE®

**Read all about the fascinating young women who lived
and loved during America's most turbulent times!**

☐ MM33156-6	**DANIELLE** Vivian Schurfranz	$2.
☐ MM33241-4	#5 **JOANNA** Jane Claypool Miner	$2.
☐ MM33242-2	#6 **JESSICA** Mary Francis Shura	$2.
☐ MM33239-2	#7 **CAROLINE** Willo Davis Roberts	$2.
☐ MM33688-6	#14 **CASSIE** Vivian Schurfranz	$2.
☐ MM33686-X	#15 **ROXANNE** Jane Claypool Miner	$2.
☐ MM41468-2	#16 **MEGAN** Vivian Schurfranz	$2.
☐ MM41438-0	#17 **SABRINA** Candice F. Ransom	$2.
☐ MM42134-4	#18 **VERONICA** Jane Claypool Miner	$2.
☐ MM40049-5	#19 **NICOLE** Candice F. Ransom	$2.
☐ MM42228-6	#20 **JULIE** Vivian Schurfranz	$2.
☐ MM40394-X	#21 **RACHEL** Vivian Schurfranz	$2.
☐ MM40395-8	#22 **COREY** Jane Claypool Miner	$2.
☐ MM40717-1	#23 **HEATHER** Vivian Schurfranz	$2.
☐ MM40716-3	#24 **GABRIELLE** Mary Francis Shura	$2.
☐ MM41000-8	#25 **MERRIE** Vivian Schurfranz	$2.
☐ MM41012-1	#26 **NORA** Jeffie Ross Gordon	$2.
☐ MM41191-8	#27 **MARGARET** Jane Claypool Miner	$2.
☐ MM41207-8	#28 **JOSIE** Vivian Schurfranz	$2.
☐ MM41416-X	#29 **DIANA** Mary Francis Shura	$2.
☐ MM42043-7	#30 **RENEE** Vivian Schurfranz	$2
☐ MM42015-1	#31 **JENNIE** Jane Claypool Miner	$2
☐ MM42016-X	#32 **DARCY** Mary Francis Shura	$2

Available wherever you buy books, or use the coupon below.

Scholastic Inc., P.O. Box 7502, 2932 East McCarty Street, Jefferson City, MO 65

Please send me the books I have checked above. I am enclosing $ _____
(please add $1.00 to cover shipping and handling). Send check or money-order—no cash or
C.O.D.'s please.

Name _____

Address _____

City _____ State/Zip _____

Please allow four to six weeks for delivery. Offer good in U.S.A. only. Sorry, mail order not availa
to residents of Canada. Prices subject to change.

SUN

The Girls of Canby Hall®

by Emily Chase

School pressures! Boy trouble! Roommate rivalry! The girls of Canby Hall are learning about life and love now that they've left home to live in a private boarding school.

1212-4	#1	Roommates	$2.50
2048-8	#2	Our Roommate Is Missing	$2.50
0080-0	#3	You're No Friend of Mine	$2.25
1417-8	#4	Keeping Secrets	$2.50
0082-7	#5	Summer Blues	$2.25
0083-5	#6	Best Friends Forever	$2.25
1277-9	#19	One Boy Too Many	$2.50
0392-3	#20	Friends Times Three	$2.25
0657-4	#21	Party Time!	$2.50
0711-2	#22	Troublemaker	$2.50
0833-X	#23	But She's So Cute	$2.50
1055-5	#24	Princess Who?	$2.50
1090-3	#25	The Ghost of Canby Hall	$2.50
1371-6	#26	Help Wanted!	$2.50
1390-2	#27	The Roommate and the Cowboy	$2.50
1516-6	#28	Happy Birthday Jane	$2.50
1671-5	#29	A Roommate Returns	$2.50
1672-3	#30	Surprise!	$2.50
1673-1	#31	Here Comes the Bridesmaid	$2.50
2149-2	#32	Who Has a Crush on Andy?	$2.50

Complete series available wherever you buy books.

Scholastic Inc.
Box 7502, 2932 East McCarty Street, Jefferson City, MO 65102

Please send me the books I have checked above. I am enclosing $_____ (please add $1.00 to cover shipping and handling). Send check or money order—no cash or C.O.D.'s please.

Name_____

Address_____

_____State/Zip_____

Please allow four to six weeks for delivery. Offer good in U.S.A. only. Sorry, mail order not available to residents of Canada. Prices subject to change.

CAN888